Fat Tuesday

Acknowledgements

Karen Davison
Harvey Thornton
Julie Drummond-Milne
Raymond Chalmers
John Thornton
Tom Chalmers
Keirsten Clark

Fat Tuesday

Gary Davison

Paperbooks Publishing Ltd
Unit 11, 63 Clerkenwell Road, London EC1M 5NP
www.paperbooks.co.uk

British Library Cataloguing in Publication Data available.

ISBN: 978-1-9062310-1-9

Set in Times
Printed by J. H. Haynes and Co. Ltd., Sparkford.

Cover designed by Chris Gooch – Bene Imprimatur Ltd

To Karen

Part One

1

Gregg's a huge kid. A bear. He's got to be over six feet and everything's in proportion: fat face, fat arms, fat belly, fat legs. He's got mousy hair that he occasionally gets cut to the bone, making his face look even fatter. I remember the first time I met him in the Traveller's Rest hostel. I'd only been backpacking for a week or so and I hadn't made any friends, and he came straight over to me in the kitchen trying to sell me a microwave meal. Honestly, I hate ravioli, but before I knew what was happening the meal was in the mic and I was a couple of dollars lighter.

That same night I started at Vasey supermarket as a shelf packer and Gregg was there with a South African lad called Cam, and we teamed up straight away. Soon after, he let me in on the scam he had going. He had one of the delivery drivers squared up to damage food that was meant for the home deliveries and he sold it to the other backpackers in the hostel for cheaps. Over time he had fine-tuned his operation and now had a decent order list that he tried to meet.

At first, I just helped smuggle the gear out, which wasn't difficult because most of it would have been binned anyway, then people got to know me in the hostel and I began delivering the food and collecting the cash while Gregg expanded his customer base to other hostels down the road.

A few weeks later, a girl I'd met on the Melbourne-to-Sydney bus started the night shift at Vaseys. Amber's about five-nine, shoulder-length brown hair, real bonny face and if she'd given me any encouragement I would have got stuck straight into her, but she didn't. I knew from the start that if I was going to get anywhere with her, it would take a lot of groundwork. Too much groundwork. That aside, she was a sound laugh and like me, unable to resist being in Gregg's company.

Within weeks, Gregg, Cam, Amber and me had moved into a flat around the corner from the Traveller's Rest. The delivery scam was working well and Amber and Cam were on board in the same capacity as me. We pooled all our money and were living like kings. Gregg incessantly looked for opportunities to expand our operation and every night was an open floor. We felt we were maximising our opportunities at the supermarket, so we tended to concentrate on our afternoon jobs.

From eleven until four, I worked at Ralf's Autos as a general dogsbody, emptying the rubbish, topping up the fridges and making sure the lids were down on the newspaper racks outside. If I found myself with nothing to do, I helped the lads in the carwash.

The owner's son was called Craig. He was nineteen, a year younger than me, and into weightlifting; with his square chin and shaven head he looked well handy. Craig hated his father because he didn't get paid much for working around the garage.

One afternoon, we were sitting on the wall taking our break, when I noticed a pattern with the customers. They would pull in, get out of their cars, look at the colour on the main fuel box, feel for the handle and fill up. Nearly every customer did this. We had another smoke and I counted eleven out of fifteen following the same agitated procedure: come on come on, things to do. Think about it. When you pull into a garage you're in a hurry, you want to fill up and get out, no hanging about, there's nothing to see. Garages are so uninteresting you'll wait until the very last second and risk conking out before doing the blasted deed of re-fuelling. In a garage you're not concentrating on what you're doing.

Craig was laying the mother of moans on me about how he never got paid a nut for working last weekend, or the one before that, or the one before that... how he would gladly top the old fucker if he thought he could get away with it.

With this in mind, I casually said, "I've got a proposition for you."

He straightened up, chin out, looking for the catch. "A proposition?"

"A proposition."

Repeating the word confused him even more, so I bowled straight in. I asked him how far a car would get if it was filled with the wrong juice. Two-kilometres max – less if it's a fuel injection, he reckoned. This was the plan. Once we selected the victim, I would switch the nozzle over on the diesel. When they pulled out, Craig would be right behind them in the recovery truck, which he uses to get to work and back every day anyway, and follow them until they break down. Then he would offer to tow them to another nearby garage and as a good turn only charge them $150.

Five minutes passed and he was still staring at me.

You can never tell with these Aussie weightlifters what's coming next, and I was suggesting we fuck with his father's business here so he could've been contemplating sticking one on me.

I was just about to ease off the wall and leg it, when he offered me a smoke.

After blowing a few smoke rings, he said, "What if they're in the NRMA or something?"

"As long as the victim's a woman, the embarrassment factor should swing it. In the city centre? Massive traffic jam? They'll jump at it. Guaranteed."

The next day, after our break, and after some ridiculous what ifs from Craig, we were ready to go. A petite brunette, mid-twenties, wearing huge black sunglasses and driving a black BMW convertible was next in line. I strolled over and wiped the side of the petrol tank. Turning my back to the camera, I casually switched the pumps over and waved a car out ahead of me before walking towards the carwash. The brunette picked up the nozzle and kept her eye on the litres. After paying, she strutted across the forecourt, dropped her shades down and stepped into her car. Craig pulled out right behind her.

Half-an-hour later I thought, he's stuck in traffic.

An hour, crashed and burned, it's come on top, we're fucked.

By the time he got back I was all for jacking in and trying for full-time at the supermarket. Craig headed towards me, walking like he had shit his pants. The closer he got, the more convinced I was that he had actually filled them to the brim. Either that or someone had taken a Stanley knife to his groin – go on son, let 'em have it!

"Nearly perfect," he said, talking out the side of his mouth.

"Nearly?"

"She broke down about half a mile away and I was right up her arse. And what an arse."

"Wasn't it just."

"Like you said, she was embarrassed, didn't bat an eye at the $150 charge."

"Nice one."

"Drops her off at that Prestige Performance garage, then she pulls out the cheque book."

"Shit!" I flicked my smoke onto the road and started

pacing. "Cheques are no good, it's a trace back to us."

"I wrote her guarantee number on the back."

I felt sorry for Craig. He thought he had done well, and he had. "It's not a problem," I said. "At least it works. We'll cash this one, but in future go via George Street and ask them if they have the money. If they don't, take them to the cashpoint. Say you'll only accept a cheque with a guarantee card but you'll have to charge full price, two-eighty."

Craig's father was in bad health and the set days he was at the hospital we planned to do the scam. Today, we decided to only try a couple more to see if there were any comebacks.

By four o'clock, I wished we'd been doing them every half-hour it was working so well. But, like Craig pointed out, the comebacks probably wouldn't happen the same day.

We split the three hundred and I raced back to the flat to tell the others.

Gregg was clattering dishes in the kitchen and Amber and Cam were watching the news.

Cam and Amber had been spending a lot of time together since we moved into the flat and it was pissing me off. I know it shouldn't and as a mate I should be happy and all that, but I'm not. Don't get me wrong, Cam's a good looking kid, blond hair in a set of curtains, slim, bony face that I know the birds go for, but – well, I saw her first, didn't I? I thought we had a connection, a little something that might take off much later. Anyway, I thought we were all meant to be mates, not getting it on.

Yesterday I had that thought. You know the one where you imagine that if the people in the room could see inside your head they'd be disgusted at what you were thinking? But I couldn't help it. And he's really started to grind on me, Amber look at this, Amber listen to this, fuck's sakes. I know it's blatant jealousy, but how do you stop it? You can't. You can pretend you're not bothered, but when someone close to you gives you the hump you can't ignore it because it's there every day right in your face.

"Evening, all," I said.

"Evening, back street guy," Cam said.

Amber leant back and lifted her hand up. "Hi, Spence."

I squeezed her hand.

Gregg emerged from the kitchen, teatowel in hand, white hairy belly poking out the bottom of his t-shirt. "Well, then? Did you give it a go?"

"Shit, I forgot," Cam said, kneeling up on the sofa.

"There were a few teething problems," I said, setting my bag down. "And Craig's arse was twitching like fuck..." I spread the notes into a fan. "But... sweet as!" Gregg dived on top of me and the other two completed the pile on. I had made nearly a week's wages in one day. In three days I'd equal roughly what we make off the delivery scam. I swear we were hysterical, rolling around the floor, piling on whoever was left on the bottom. This was a major breakthrough. Fucking major!

The doorbell interrupted our celebrations. We froze, entangled on the floor. Gregg crept over to the window. I don't know why we were so stunned, probably because we never got any visitors, apart from takeaway delivery drivers. Gregg gripped the flaky windowsill and peered down. My arm was still around Amber's waist. The three of us stirred and she swiftly removed it.

"Who is it?" I whispered.

Gregg held his hand up.

"It's okay, he's gone," he sighed. "Fat bloke, big ginger beard, suit jacket. I think it might have been a tax inspector."

"Why do we have to hide from a tax inspector?" I asked.

"Because I'm claiming I live here alone, that way we get a twenty-five percent rebate on the rates." Gregg had a grin from ear to ear as he watched me gather the notes up and drop them into the tin. "That's a tremendous day's work, Spence. You didn't even have to do that much graft. Not like me, running around like a nutter."

I sat in the bay window looking out over the treetops into the park. I got thinking about different stuff and, well, the truth is, if I'm being honest, what I really needed was a girl. Trouble is, I got on so well with

Amber, and… and… I'm fucked if I know. I'm not in love with her or anything. Christ, we'd only been mates seven weeks or something, it's just… there's something there and each day I'm watching it slip further away.

"You okay, Spence?" Amber said, kneeling in front of me. "You're not worried about any problems after today, are you?"

"Nah, it went spot on. We're keeping the reg numbers of the cars so we don't do anyone twice, so it should be sweet."

She stood up, using my knee for leverage and I got a waft of blackcurrant from her lips. Her lips are perfect and her mouth wide, like Julia Roberts, and she's constantly glossing up with juicy tubes. Whenever she settles down on the sofa or you stop and talk to her at work, the juicy tube comes out and she glosses up and pouts. Today's flavour was blackcurrant and I could almost feel her kissing me.

Fuck's sakes, I wish I could get my head round this. I've waited so long to have real friends, and here I am wishing the worst on one of them and leching over the other.

Gregg had been pacing around the flat and was now hovering behind my chair. I asked him what was up and he nodded towards his room. I followed him over.

He unravelled a roll of paper about a metre long onto his bed, weighing each corner down with shoes and his bedside clock. He stood in front of the bed, towering over me, and said, "This is strictly between you and me."

I nodded and he stepped aside.

It was a construction drawing of the supermarket. "What the fuck? Where did you get this?"

"Nicked it off Jeff, the maintenance bloke."

The robbery of a supermarket was something you heard about on the news or saw in a film, or fantasised about when you were twenty-year-old scamsters like us. Looking at the drawing made it feel too real. I knew how Gregg operated and if I gave this the green light, we'd be on the brink of doing it within a week.

"Hey," Gregg said. "Don't worry, we're only exploring the possibilities like we said."

For the first time, he was looking for approval and he had turned to me. Not Cam. Me. Fuck Cam, he was moving in on Amber and if I got my way he'd be out the door.

"One thing," I said, straightening up. "Whatever we do about this from now on, we do together. No gathering information, maps or fuck all else, unless we both agree. That way, if we do decide to go ahead neither can blame the other for making a mistake."

I sounded like I knew what I was on about, but I just didn't want this getting out of hand. Gregg was a dreamer and this would probably never come off, but I didn't want us getting nicked in the meantime because he went delving in without any real thought about what he was doing.

Gregg's so thick-skinned that if you catch the fucker out, he'll just smile or half-laugh and walk away, and it feels like he's lugged an arm over your shoulders and said, "you know it makes sense."

"Agreed," he said, smiling.

We shook on it and he kept hold of my hand and yanked me towards him.

I pointed at the damp coming through the walls in the corner of the room. "You want to get onto the landlord about that."

"Already have. I'm withholding half of next month's rent if it's not sorted."

Cam poked his head in. "What you two lovers up to?"

"You're having a laugh, aren't you?" Gregg said. "Listening to that eighties shite."

Cam gave him the finger and returned to the living room. I went to get dressed for work.

2

That night at work I couldn't stop thinking about the robbery. Apart from the secure area, we had access to the whole of the supermarket, and even if we got caught there, as employees an excuse for accidentally being out of bounds wouldn't be hard to find. With careful planning and Gregg's ability to get just about any information we needed, we could pull it off. Imagine the buzz walking out of here with all that cash...

I stood up. What the fuck was I thinking? If we got caught we'd get sent down for years. It wasn't the money. You see, the problem is, I'm holding back on the others. I don't want to, but I have to.

Eight weeks ago my father died, leaving me everything. A week later I was off backpacking. I know that looks callous, but I'd been planning it for years to escape him and the stigma he had drowned us in. My father had no real friends, only arse-lickers who worked for him, and I was destined to be his heir, but I'd fought against it my whole life.

Back home in Newcastle, I'd always been discriminated against for being the little rich kid. Even at twenty I'm still the little rich kid back there, except now I'm seriously loaded. My mother, I'm told, was working-class, which is where the main differences were between my father and me. He detested the working-class, yet he married one of them and half-raised his kid as working-class, then decided to play God and try and change things when my mother went. He was a nasty bastard, my father – not physically – but he knew how to hurt you.

Anyway, when he was diagnosed with lung cancer and his death was imminent, I had a choice. Stay in Newcastle, learn the ropes in the finance world, take over his company and be worshipped by pricks only after my money, or fuck off and start afresh, on my own, see what the world has to offer, make new friends and see where it leads me.

I didn't want to be a sneaky fucker and go behind people's back, but how could I tell my new mates that I was loaded and I came from that background and still keep things going the way they were? Pulling together and making extra coin is what we're all about. If I tell them I'm not skint like them it'll spoil all that and believe me, no matter what they say, like everyone I've met before, they'll look at me differently, and I'll never be accepted as the same as them. AND I AM. I'm my mother's son, not that bastard's. So until we've been through enough for them not to care, I'm keeping shtum.

Gregg knelt down next to me, sharing my piece of cardboard.

"You won't fucking believe what I've just seen."

"What?"

"You know the taxman. The one at the door this afternoon? Fat fucker in the suit jacket?"

"Yeah." I sat back on my honkers.

"He's been in here for the last ten minutes."

"So. It's a supermarket." I continued packing. Tax inspectors didn't follow people to work.

"And he's been taking photos of *you*. How does he even know you live at the flat?"

"Taking pictures of me?" Gregg nodded. "He can't be a tax inspector," I said. "Are you sure he was only taking shots of me?"

"Positive, he was crouched down next to the bread. I came straight over but he was away." He lowered his head and hissed, "They're on to us already! We haven't even started planning the robbery and they're onto us!"

"Of course they're not. If they were, it would be easier to sack us."

"You're right. Well, who was it?" He titled his head back. "That's him! He's next in line to be served. Tell Aileen I've gone home sick, I'm going to follow the fucker."

The only people that might be interested in me would have something to do with my father. I've got nothing to do with running his business, so even if my father had fucked someone over, what good would it do following me all the way out here?

I carried on packing, laughing to myself.

On the way home, I filled the others in on Gregg's spying mission.

It was three in the morning when the downstairs door slammed shut and Gregg came bounding up the stairs.

He tossed his jacket onto the armchair. "That fucker is a right weirdo," he panted.

"What was he up to, then?" I said. "And why was he taking a photo of me?"

"Haven't a clue. He's staying three blocks away on Palmer Street, number 154."

"So what took you so long if he only lives three blocks away?" Amber asked.

"First up, he leaves Vaseys and heads down Crown Street and into that gay club, Columbian, on the corner of Oxford. Filthy bastard was in there for two hours. I sat in Hungry Jack's forcing a double meal down my neck."

"That'll be right," Cam scoffed.

"Then he walked straight past ours and up to The Cross and into World Bar, and I'm ducking into doorways like a nutter. After that he heads back to Palmer. He's staying in a B&B. Fuck knows what he's after but I say we keep an eye on him."

All through his story, Gregg addressed Amber and Cam. Even when he passed me the joint, he wouldn't look at me.

Cam stood up and ran his hands through his hair. "So, what else have you got for us? What's this special treat you've been banging on about all week?"

Gregg rummaged through his jacket pocket and brought out a thin piece of paper, about the size of a cigarette, perforated into six, each with a smiley face. "Now, this will get the weekend started."

"Where the hell did you get acid?" Cam said, examining the paper strip. "I haven't seen any in years."

Before I came backpacking the only thing I'd experimented with was cigarettes. It wasn't that I didn't want to try anything else, I just didn't have anyone to do it with. Acid sounded a right laugh and according to Gregg there were no drawbacks, but Cam said the stomach cramps coming down from it were a bit naughty, "but well worth it". As long as there were no long-term effects like getting addicted to the stuff, I was up for giving it a shot.

Amber was worried about not being able to stop the effect of the acid if she didn't like it.

"I'll tell you what," I said. "I'll take a half and you take a half. If we like it we'll have some more, if not, it'll soon wear off." She was thinking about it. "Come on, we're off all weekend."

"Yeah, but how long does it last? And I thought we were going to Bondi tomorrow? Lisa's reserved tickets for us for the beach party. I can't let her down. Her hostel's putting the beer on and everything."

"We can still go," Gregg said. "We'll be sound by then."

Amber loved Bondi and was always on about moving out there, but we wouldn't because we needed to be close to all the hostels for the delivery scam.

"So we're definitely going?"

We all nodded.

"I'll take a half, but no more."

3

Gregg reckoned the best way to get started on the acid was to watch a film. An animated one if we had it. *Men in Black* was the best we could do. We sat back, curtains drawn, apprehensively looking around at each other.

An hour later we were still waiting for the gear to kick in.

I went to the toilet.

The sink swayed and the orange and black striped curtains rippled, the colours mixing together. I dropped to my knees, head in my hands. I slowly opened my fingers and the rug was curling at the edges and rolling up to my legs. I fast-crawled to the sink, pulled myself up and turned the taps on. I looked in the mirror, then scarpered back into the living room.

I lay face down on the floor, arms wrapped around my head.

The train was heading my way, chugging along, getting louder, letting off steam as my head formed the tunnel. The ride was getting rough, here it comes, nearly there, Jesus it's big, shiny steel, nearly there...

Gregg was shaking me.

"You twat," he said. "You put the shits right up me. I

thought you were a goner."

We rolled around the floor laughing, knocking cups over, everything a blur, table legs bending in and out, the fireplace a face with glowing teeth and black hair.

I staggered into the kitchen, opened the fridge, then slammed it shut.

I kept on the move, half covering my face with my hand, falling over, laughing and wrestling with Gregg, who had a terrifying grin, like The Joker.

…I was on my bed, face down, squirming. Amber joined me, but I didn't want her to see my face. I stretched over and tried to eject the CD but couldn't. I turned over and jerked my head back, trying to focus. Cam gently held my face and tried to kiss me. I shoved him away and fell back over onto the floor.

Cam left the room.

I climbed back onto the bed and held on…

* * *

A piercing scream brought me to and I wobbled to the bedroom door.

"Shit!" I rushed over to Gregg. "What's happened?"

His head was hanging limp, blood dripping off his chin.

"Gregg! What's happened?"

He whispered, "She… she attacked me."

"Cam! Phone a fucking ambulance!"

I sat Gregg down and lifted his head up. There were

tiny bits of green glass embedded in his face and hands. His eyes were rolling and he was clutching an empty cigarette box in his right hand. I was still tripping and had to stop looking at his face.

I walked over to the window as the ambulance pulled up.

I guided Gregg down the stairs. They laid him on a stretcher and put an oxygen mask over his face. I told them what we had taken.

Cam got in the ambulance with him.

I waited until the ambulance had turned the corner before heading back inside.

The bathroom door was still locked.

"Amber, it's Spence. You okay?"

"I just w-want to get my stuff and leave."

"Come on, don't be daft. It's just an accident, it's the acid."

The living room was a right mess – coffee table over, glass everywhere, cups on the floor, potpourri scattered over the armchair.

"Things won't seem so bad when we all get back to normal," I said. "Gregg's just got a few cuts and bruises. I take it you two fell out?"

She was running the tap. "It's not just Gregg," she sobbed. "I've always had this trouble, you don't understand."

I heard Amber slump to the floor and lean back against the bath. I couldn't make out everything she was saying, but she was beating herself up about leaving her sister. I was still tripping, nothing too heavy, but I was having a little fun with a cigarette box during the long silences.

"What's your sister like?"

"Emma's great, Spence, she's only fifteen, wants to go travelling as well. But I should n-never have left her. Ah, Spence, what have I done? I shouldn't be here."

"Course you should. You can't live your life round your sister. I bet she's just getting on with things. You keep in touch, don't you?"

"Not as much as I should."

She was on a proper downer and talking her round from behind the bathroom door was a big ask. We sat silent again. The cigarette box. Light and dark blue, expanding and contracting. This acid's great. I'd recommend it to anyone. It's not working so much now at long range. I have to really focus, bringing things in close. I stare hard, challenging it not to work, but it's still there. Take my fingers. Arm outstretched the ends are sort of moving, close in they're like proper fat sausages, gently throbbing, and the nails are... are what? Like, say, Smith's square crisps. Looking in the mirror earlier was well tricky, but now I've got a hold of it I reckon it'll be a right laugh.

"What about your folks, Spence?" Amber said, blowing her nose. "You hardly mention them."

"You lot don't talk about home much, either. I thought that's how backpackers went on."

I shouldn't be bothered about home, but like I've said, I'm worried what they'll think until they get to know me better. At the same time, I didn't want to sound like a queer fucker and be all secretive.

"What do you want to know?"

"Tell me something about yourself – about you. Something I don't know."

"And you'll tell me something about you, I take it."

"All right."

"Eh… let me see. Let… me… see. Okay. My mother died when I was seven."

After a long pause, she dramatically said, "Spence, I'm *so* sorry."

"It's all right. I can't remember much about her to be honest. Just bits."

"Like what?"

"She was average height, had black hair like me. Argued constantly with my father."

We fell silent again.

I drifted off, thinking about my mother and home.

Our house has five double bedrooms, a double garage and a tarmac driveway big enough to park ten cars or more. My bedroom is on the first floor and I have two floor-to-ceiling windows. One looks out over the lawn and driveway, and the other gives you a view of Mill Lane, which leads to St George's Primary. I spent so much time at those windows watching my mother and father arguing.

"We've been through all this, Richard!" Mam screamed at father.

I jumped down from the window and crept over to my bedroom door.

"Please, *enlighten me*, as to why you don't want to give your only son the best education available to him? Instead you want him thrown in with the rogues and losers."

"Rogues! My whole family went to St George's! You've got some *bloody* nerve!"

"Ninety percent of them in that school will work as hired help. But that would be fine by you, wouldn't it? 'Salt of the earth'. My son will be doing the hiring –"

A door slammed.

I tiptoed back to the window, climbed up and watched Mam pacing along the front of the house smoking. She always smoked when they argued. They always argued. I tapped on the window, but she couldn't hear me. Father walked past her, shoulders back, his big man walk she called it. He has longish grey hair and always wears a blue pinstriped suit. He's much taller than Mam. I wanted to tell them that it didn't matter to me. I'd go to any school, as long as they stopped fighting.

One day, about a year-and-a-half after starting at St George's, a woman not much older than Mam came to pick me up. She introduced herself as Aunty Pat. She was taller than Mam and her face was wrinkly around her mouth and eyes. She had grey and black hair pulled tight in a ponytail. She looked like a Red Indian's wife. She told me that Mam couldn't pick me up from school this week.

"She's not too well, Spencer, as you know."

"What's wrong with her? Is she in bed?" I looked up at my window as we passed the side of the house, but she wasn't there. When we got inside, there was no sandwich on the kitchen bench. The house was quiet.

"Now then," Aunty Pat said, kneeling in front of me. She unhooked my satchel and began loosening my tie. "What do you usually do with your mam at this time?"

Aunty Pat was great, even better than Mam. She let me hang about next to the fence and talk with the other kids coming home – not that Mam stopped me, but if my father ever came in early, which was never, it made things difficult and they argued, but Aunty Pat didn't seem to care what Father thought.

A few days later, Aunty Pat took me to the hospital in town. It was busy and hot, everyone pushing past me. The horrible smell of ointment made me feel sick. We went into a private room and Aunty Pat shut the door. I looked up at Mam, but she was asleep. Aunty Pat lifted me onto the bed. Mam looked pale and old and she had a bright green bit of jelly on the side of her mouth. She woke up, smiled, and held my hand. Her hand was sweaty and her fingers longer than normal. I leaned in to try and hear what she was saying, but couldn't. She smelled and I wanted to go back home. I could see why she couldn't pick me up from school.

By the time we got back, it was too late to go outside so I went up to my room and watched for anyone coming along Mill Lane.

It was dark when I heard Father's car pull up. I switched to the front window, but they were too close to the house for me to see. Aunty Pat walked up the driveway. Halfway up, she turned and waved and blew me a kiss. I kept on waving until she disappeared behind the tree.

"Spence? You okay?"

"Yeah, sound. I think this gear's wearing off."

I walked over to the window. No sign of the others. I went to the kitchen and returned with a glass of water. Amber was still in the bathroom.

"How you feeling?" I asked.

"Like I want to kill myself. I can't believe what's happened. I thought all this was behind me, but things never go away. Never!" She kicked the bath. "It's n-not my fault."

"Take it easy. I've told you, no one will blame you. He's only got a few little cuts. We were all stoned."

I picked the cigarette box up again but the acid had worn off. I could see a slight movement, but nothing like before. I wouldn't mind a little top up – not a full half, maybe a quarter just to get tripping again. After the hysteria stage, which has its pluses too, Gregg and me had a right laugh, tripping when you're in control is unreal.

"You'll never trust me again," Amber snivelled. "Trust, Spence. You've got to have that, haven't you?"

"Of course I trust you. We all do."

"You see, that's why I fell out with my mam. I couldn't trust her. She let me down."

"How come?"

She didn't answer.

I tried to talk her from behind the door, but she kept breaking down, banging on about trust and how trust was what everything was built on. Everytime I suggested something she went off on one.

The trust thing bothered me. I didn't want to be like my father and let people down. I didn't want to tell lies. If I'd known she wouldn't change towards me, I'd have told her straight away. But what happens when we're all sober and Amber looks across at me; does she see Spence the shelf-packer or a twenty-year-old millionaire playing at being normal?

I cleared my throat. "My father died not long back."

Amber stopped snivelling.

"Spence," she whispered. "No folks. And here I am whingeing about mine. I'm so sorry. I really am. I couldn't imagine. Don't," she paused. "Don't you have anyone?"

"Cousins. An aunt and uncle, but I never see them. I've never been one for needing loads of people around me, and my father and me didn't get on anyway."

After a few minutes, she said, "I love you, Spence."

I thought about what she had just said. I love you Spence.

There are two types of love. The let's be best friends go to the flicks flirty kissing on lips with no tongues share problems love, and the tear each other's clothes off inseparable for life love. I wished to fuck it was the second, but right now I'd take either to be with Amber.

"I'm not just saying it because of this, you know. It's not the drugs and that. I really do. I trust you. I have since we met on the bus and I don't trust people easy, you know that."

I went to the kitchen and made us both a tea.

When I returned, Amber was sat on the sofa. I handed her the cup.

She didn't look up. "Thanks."

Her face was puffed up and spotty. Her hair matted to the side of her head.

Our eyes met and she burst into tears.

"It's not my f-fault, it's not my fault, it's not my fault."

"I don't blame you, neither will anyone else."

Stroking her hair and saying nothing did the trick and she cried herself out. I felt so sorry for her. I wished I could have said something, I mean, she was at it so hard she could hardly breathe.

I eased her head off my chest, held her neck and slid my arm under her knees. On the count of three, I lifted her up and staggered towards her room. Fuck me, she was heavy. I bounced off the door, lost my footing and we landed in a heap. She woke up and started bubbling.

"I'm sorry," I was saying, trying to retrieve my arms, "not a safe landing. Hold on… you're laughing, aren't you?"

"Ah, Spence! I can't believe you even attempted it!"

"It's not over yet."

"You're not big enough!"

"Get your hand round my neck, here we go, lift!" I stumbled into her room and we fell forward onto the bed, laughing.

After we recovered, Amber edged away and I felt uncomfortable lying so close to her.

I went back in the room to wait for the others.

I was sitting up, chain-smoking, when the lads arrived back. Cam looked scared, hands shaking, eyes flashing round the room. I don't think the acid agreed with him at all. Gregg's face was covered in cuts, his lips swollen, butterfly stitches on his arm. He told me about the hospital trauma, then glanced over at Amber's door. "Honest to God, I don't even think I made lip contact before she went off it. And I mean *off it*. I thought you lot had joined in. I'm not fucking joking, she kicked me all over."

I walked over, lightly knocked on her door and went in. "Fancy another cuppa?"

She nodded. "My stomach's in agony."

"Tell me about it." I walked to the door. "Come on, the lynch mob are waiting."

Amber came out and trudged over to the sofa.

Gregg winked at her. "I take it that's a definite no, then?"

4

Cam and Gregg were standing toe-to-toe arguing like fuck about the robbery of Vasey supermarket, when I got a flashback of Cam holding my face and trying to kiss me. I was stunned. I contemplated it not being real, but it was too vivid.

Watching him now, I'm wondering how I didn't suss him out before. When he's talking he's all hands, when he's listening it's hands on hips, and when he sits down after Gregg has browbeaten him into submission, he theatrically crosses his legs and hooks his hair behind his ears. I swear he couldn't look more bent if he tried.

Last night, when we were stoned, I let it slip about the robbery. I'd also forgotten that I had, so Gregg and I had been put on the spot without a chance to make up a defence. The bottom line was, we didn't know if it was possible to rob Vaseys. All we were asking for was a chance to look into it. A little research to see how difficult it would be.

"If we don't all agree," Cam was saying, "then we don't do it. I don't want to be railroaded into this."

"We know, we know. Make yourself useful and draw the curtains." Gregg replaced the mirror over the fireplace with the layout of the supermarket.

Cam leapt up, pointing at the drawing. "I thought you said we were just talking about it! You can get sent down for conspiracy just for that! Look, Gregg, I don't think you've considered the consequences of this. If a rozza walked through that door, we'd all go to prison *right now*! That's before we even do anything. And for what? A few dollars. Do we really need to do this?"

The secure area was located to the right of the checkouts as you walked through the main entrance doors. Cashiers occasionally carried their own tills beyond the mirror-panelled doors when helping out a supervisor or a key colleague (a key colleague overlooked a smaller area of the shopfloor, but still had a certain amount of authority). Both had access to the secure area, and if one of us could get on till duty, we might get a look inside. We also needed to take care of the security cameras and, according to Gregg, the CCTV room would be next to the safe office.

"It might not be," Amber said. "It could be in those rooms at the back of the warehouse."

Gregg pointed to the rooms Amber was referring to on the drawing. "That one there's Jeff's office. That's where I got this plan."

"How did you manage that?" Cam asked.

"Stuck my head in to offer him some microwave meals but he was at the bog, so I rolled it up and shoved it down the inside leg of my pants."

"Must have been a tight squeeze," I said.

"Very funny, puny boy," he said, patting his gut. "Anyway, I'm on a diet."

We needed to know for sure the layout inside the secure area and how the doors were opened, and who had access. One person who might have keys to the surveillance room was Jeff.

"If there's a serious fault, they get an outside company in on standby to fix it," Gregg said. "Jeff hates them, thinks it undermines his position, but the little stuff he sorts himself, so he must have access to the back rooms."

"Not unless a supervisor takes him in," I said.

"He's got all sorts in that office and he never works after twelve, so if we get his keys we could have a spy on our break."

We agreed to try Jeff's office on Monday and Amber was going to apply for till duty.

5

I own over seventy per cent of my father's company, Hargreaves Financial. The company today is run like it was when my father was alive, with the entire senior staff still in place. Howard Buckley, the head company accountant, and Peter Simms, the family solicitor, both close friends of my father's, offered me their services on a personal level when my father died.

I never thought I would need to call them, but the bloke taking photos of me in the supermarket had bothered me. I couldn't get the fucker out my mind and I was sure it had something to do with home. I'd thought about going over to Palmer Street and confronting him, but that could draw even more attention to me, so I was going to find out what he was up to, then decide what to do.

Peter Simms is always very official with me, so I went for Howard Buckley.

Buckley is an old fashioned number cruncher, who is always hunched over his desk tapping away on his calculator or squinting at his computer monitor. I've never seen him walk, but I imagine he can only walk in the seated position – a human chair, a red beanbag on stumpy legs with a rashy face that only gets shaved once a month. Buckley's not a drinker, I don't think, just a junk food addict. He's in his late-forties, but looks sixty and for someone who generally doesn't give a fuck what he dresses or smells like, he takes a lot of pride in combing a few black strands over his rashy nut.

I lay back on my bed and dialled his direct number.

"Howard Buckley."

"Hi Howard, it's Spencer. You okay?"

"Spencer, my boy! How are you! The Scarlet Pimpernel! How come you never return any calls?"

"Probably because you never leave any messages."

"I hate technology. You know that. If I had my way it would all still be done on paper. Every week there's new software on the market, and the powers that be insist we use them. As if life in this sector isn't difficult enough."

This would go on forever if I didn't step in. "Look, Howard, I'm after a favour."

He went quiet.

"You still there?"

"Of course. Go on. A favour, yes. What can I do for you?"

"I think I'm being followed. I know I am."

"Followed? In Australia?"

"I'm sure of it."

"By whom?"

"I've no idea. That's what I want you to find out."

"You think it's someone from home?"

"Got to be."

"That's absurd! You're on the other side of the world!"

I waited for the Father Christmas laugh he was putting on to die down.

"I can always ask someone else, Howard, if it's too much hassle. What about the MD, Mike Jones? He'll know if anyone's got grievances with my father, because that's all it can be."

"No, no. Leave it with me. Jones is hopeless. He's only in it for himself. God knows why your father left him in the driving seat.

"Everything is going fine here, Spencer, as I'm sure Peter Simms has told you. I'll make a few calls, see if anyone's been pushing hard recently and get back to you. Chances are, it's nothing. What does this man look like?"

I told him.

"Can't see anyone going to these lengths, Spencer, I really can't. I'll be in touch."

"Cheers, Howard."

The line went dead. Outside my bedroom door I heard footsteps scurrying away and down the stairs. The front door crashed shut.

I paced the living room trying to conjure up an excuse, but the only explanation I could think of was the truth. I flopped onto the armchair, resting one foot up on the windowsill. Fuck's sakes, I wish I had just come out with it, but then what? Back to Newcastle? I know this is a fine line I'm treading and no one trusts a liar, but what else can I do? What other options do I have?

They're probably sitting in the park right now, figuring out how to deal with someone that might be being followed. The ball gets rolling and they see me as someone they can't trust. A stranger that no longer fits in.

When I was young, my father did everything he could to ensure I didn't fit in. The fucker knew I only had one mate and he even tried to fuck that up for me by keeping me away from him to further my education. I swear, I could be sick now thinking about that summer and it could be happening all over again.

A new nanny was starting and I had everything planned: be good, show her how much I loved schoolwork, and then down to the park to meet Wayne. Wayne Clements was in my class at St George's. He wasn't bothered about the other kids, he was happy it just being me and him. That's the way I liked it, and the other kids didn't bother with us, except when we were in class or playing football. Wayne and me both played on the left and in two years' time we'd be old enough to play for the under-tens.

I'd been to Wayne's house once, but kept it from my father. I knew he wouldn't approve. All my father was interested in was schoolwork and more schoolwork.

The morning the new nanny was due to start, Father sat me down at the kitchen table and told me that I was going to be getting extra tuition after school.

"But why?"

"Spencer, you know I didn't want you to go to St George's."

"But I'm doing well. Wayne and me."

"Never mind Wayne. I'm sure he's a very nice lad but he's not destined for the same career as you." He took a bite out of his toast and crossed his long legs. "Your mother and I fought about which school you should go to and I regret not sticking to my guns. So extra tuition, young man, is the only way to get you up to speed, because they'll not be at this level in your next school."

I nodded and continued eating my cereal.

"In each and every subject."

I didn't look up.

"Starting tonight at four sharp. So no dawdling on the way home. Margaret knows to get you straight here, so no tricks with her either. You hear?"

I jumped up and ran out the kitchen.

"Spencer! Come back here!"

I knew he wouldn't come after me.

So, for five nights a week I couldn't play out. Couldn't sit at the back of the tennis courts with Wayne. What would he say? He'd probably find a new friend. I sat in the window watching everyone heading into school. Wayne usually came to the corner and whistled, and I would head straight down. Without Wayne I'd have no one.

It was a sunny day and we had games on the top field. Usually I'd be looking forward to it, but all I could think about was the extra schoolwork. Why did I have to do extra when I'd done okay at school? I nearly started to cry, but held it in. My chest hurt. What about the summer holidays? The scheme at the park opened at the start of the holidays and it was *the* place to be. First thing in the morning they'd open the community centre up, which also doubled as changing rooms for the local pub football teams. All our stuff was at the other end, away from the showers. Last year we were too young to join in all the games, it was mostly for the older lads, some nearly sixteen-years-old, but this year we'd be able to play in most of them. We'd get first choice on swing ball, tennis rackets, water pistols, skateboards, and we'd have our names up for five-a-side and the assault course. Maybe not the assault course, but we'd get a shot at just about everything else.

The second nanny I had that year was really cool. She was younger than the others, someone from Father's office. I don't think she was really a nanny, and she stayed over a lot compared to the others. But she let me go down to the park straight after school and always got me back in time and in bed before he came in. If she was here I'd have no trouble getting down the park all day in the summer holidays.

The next two weeks were hell. The tutors I got were horrible. Mr Blake was the worst. He was old with grey hair and a short beard, and smelt of pipe smoke and farts. I had to cup my hands over my nose when he leant in and wrote on the notepad.

"This should be familiar ground for you, Spencer. The point here is for me to see what level you are at. You understand."

I nodded.

"Take your hands from your mouth, please, so I can hear what you're saying."

By the time the tutors had finished with me, it was hardly worth sitting in the window as everyone had already passed along Mill Lane.

Every morning at school became more and more unbearable as Wayne told me what I had missed out on. He had also started to hang around with John Ellis, who was in the year above us. John Ellis was much taller than us and had a really long face, like a Great Dane dog, and his mouth eased open without him even knowing it. During school time, he had started to nod at me when I passed him, and eventually began to talk, even though he was only boasting about what Wayne and he had been doing.

One break time, the three of us were standing at the bottom of the playground stairs. John Ellis was showing us a Kinger ball bearing he had won playing marbles. He probably had the biggest collection of marbles in the school and hardly ever brought them all in. He dropped a few out of his cloth moneybag onto the grass behind the wall and said we could choose one each. I hesitated.

"Go on then," he said. "What's the matter? They not good enough for you?"

"No, it's not that. I was just letting Wayne have first bats."

"It's because you're a snob, Hargreaves. Right up yourself. My dad reckons your dad looks down on us."

"It's not true. Just because we've got extra."

"It's true," Wayne said, holding a marble up so the sun reflected through it. "I heard Mam and Dad talking about him, says he didn't even wave when they let him through with his car. Stuck up." The whistle sounded and I was pushed along towards the assembly hall doorway.

The summer holidays were nearly here. I had seen my father at breakfast most days and kept my head down, hoping the tuition wasn't going to continue. I couldn't stand it. I tried to grasp what they were saying, hoping that he would see I'd done well, but he never said I had.

He folded his newspaper and dropped it onto his briefcase. "Mr Blake tells me the effort is there. In a few years this will seem a normal level of work to you. It's all about self-discipline." He turned to Margaret, who'd just arrived in the kitchen, clutching her brown handbag tight to her side. Margaret looked like a grandma off TV. She had curly white hair and wore brown tights and drab clothes that were too hot for summer. No wonder oldies smelled so much.

Father pointed at me. "Make sure he's back straight after school. The scholar needs his practice."

My father had been so chirpy since I'd started the extra classes, but he wasn't bothered that I was missing out on so many other things. I tried to tell him and promised to work harder at school, but he wouldn't listen. It wasn't fair, not being allowed out at night.

Today was the last day of school. Tomorrow, the community scheme started. Mrs Snowdon, the headmistress, briefed the whole school at assembly about safety and good behaviour. She said the scheme was operated on a year-to-year basis and could easily be moved to another area if it wasn't successful. No one was listening. All I could think about was the extra things we could do compared to last year. Five-a-side, tennis, you name it, we'd be in it. Extra work or not, he couldn't keep me away from there all day.

Wayne came up to me after assembly and he looked white. Like he might puke.

"What's up?"

He shook his head. "We're going away for the summer."

"What? How long? When? Where to?"

"Scotland to see Dad's sister."

I had to stop myself crying. Then I had to stop my temper from getting up. What was I going to do?

Wayne put an arm around my shoulder. "Don't worry.

John'll still be here. You two are mates now. How do you think I feel, missing everything?"

Wayne had to leave school at lunchtime. I tried to speak to John Ellis, to arrange a meet for tomorrow, but he was always too busy with older lads.

I sat on a wall and watched some lads playing marbles. One had a huge clothbag full to the top, and he had the biggest ball bearing I'd ever seen. When I followed the game along the grass, he half-turned to warn me off. The others did the same. They were older than me so I guess it was okay. It wasn't cool to be seen with younger lads.

When the bell sounded for home time, I caught up with John Ellis at the gates.

"See you down there tomorrow, John."

"Yeah, see you there. Wayne coming?"

I didn't get a chance to answer. He was off with a couple of mates.

Margaret was standing on the other side of the road (a little deal we had going on), waiting to take me home.

My father wasn't at breakfast the following morning, but he had told Margaret to make sure I'd done the extra homework before letting me out to play. Tuition was continuing throughout the summer, although only every other night. This didn't seem so bad with Wayne being away, and hopefully, I would have done enough extra work to stop all together by the time he got back.

I finished the homework by ten and got changed into my shorts and t-shirt. Margaret made me a packed lunch, which I shoved into my bag with my strip and football boots. She insisted on walking me to the park and threatened to come right down and get me if I wasn't at the gates to be picked up by three o'clock. I sat under a tree, in the shade.

The park was packed with people playing football, tennis, netball, rounders, swing ball – you name it. And there were loads of groups hanging around, sitting in circles, waiting to get on things. To the left of the community centre was a half-blown-up bouncy castle, and the workers were putting the assault course out alongside it. The skateboarders were rocketing down the footpath and throwing themselves off at the bottom near the bouncy castle. If Wayne had been here, we would have ran straight over and put our names up for everything.

I spotted John Ellis and my heart skipped a beat. He was on his way back up the footpath carrying his skateboard.

I sat for half-an-hour watching, before heading down. I walked towards the main entrance looking out for people I knew, but even those in my class hardly noticed me. When you're playing, you don't notice people. There were two lots of football nets up at the goals behind the centre. Wayne and me would have just taken a ball and played on the back of them.

The door was open, people running in and out. The

smell of ointment from the football changing rooms hit me as I walked in. A few footballers side-stepped me and ran out, their studs rattling on the pavement as they made for the pitch. Everyone seemed to be into something. I wished I had been here at the start.

"Hi!" A lady in purple jogging bottoms bounced towards me. Her blonde hair was held back with a thick red band across her forehead and she had big round glasses on that made her brown eyes look like flattened conkers. "Now, I know you! You're Spencer! How are you?"

"I'm okay."

"Right then! What can we put you down for?"

I signed up for five-a-side, which was due to start soon. I was really nervous, but I'd be okay once I started playing.

I walked out of the building and along towards the corner, where they were coming down the path on skateboards. To my right there were five-a-side goals – with nets! With nets! I couldn't believe it. Imagine hitting one straight into the top corner. I spotted John Ellis talking to a few lads, all a lot taller than him, and miles taller than me, but they had football boots on. I sat on the kerb and put mine on and pushed my socks down a bit and trotted over. I took a deep breath and tapped John on the side. "Hey, I think I'm playing in –"

A lad turned around. "Hey what, pip? You think what?" He was huge and even had stubble. He must have been at least twenty-five. Long dark hair covered one side of his face. He had a black and blue striped strip on.

The rest turned to look at me.

I tilted my head up at John, who looked tiny compared to these lads. "What's up? I think I'm in your team for the five-a-side." I went to walk towards him, but one of the older lads heel-slapped me in the forehead and I went flying. It was okay. It was to be expected. All younger lads get heel-slapped. It meant nothing. As I pushed myself up and staggered forward, I heard my name.

The longhaired one shoved me into the middle. "So you're Hargreaves? Little Tommy reckons you're minted. Proper toff."

All the faces were looking down and laughing. I made a lunge towards John, but he pushed me back in.

"He's fucking loaded. Our Stevey reckons he gets shagged off all the nannies."

"Is that right? You get shagged off the nannies?"

"Nanny shagger!"

"His fatha shags the nannies. Even the old ones! I bet he fuckin shags you. Does he? Eh?"

"Nanny shagger!"

"Nanny shagger!"

"Nanny shagger!"

"Where's y'mother Nanny shagger?"

"Spoilt fucker!"

It got blurred. I couldn't see anyone. I kept getting to my feet and bouncing off them. I crawled to one side, but they kicked me back into the middle. I got my temper up and tried not to cry. I ran at them hard, but it made it worse and they took my arms and legs and started giving me the bumps, throwing me so high I could see rooftops.

"Break it up! Stop that right now!"

I was lying face down. My shirt had been torn off. I stumbled to my feet and pulled my shorts up. Everyone was watching. The woman took my hand, but I broke free and started to run.

"Spencer, come back!" she shouted. "It's best if you stay, really!"

Head down, I ran past the skateboarders.

I reached the top, holding it in, and kept on running.

* * *

I sat in the bay window, looking out over the park. The others were due back soon.

I didn't want to spend the rest of my life living a lie, but how could I free myself of my past? If I told them too soon, before we'd been through enough together, it wouldn't work out. They'd see me as a different breed to them, but I'm not. I detest everything my father stood for. Money, power, social standing. Means fuck all to me. He discriminated against the working-class like they were a different species. He couldn't see people as individuals. And what did he have in the end that they didn't? A shit load of money, no friends and a son who hated him. He died a lonely man. Got what he deserved if you ask me.

I just didn't want to go the same way. I wanted a chance to live my life the way I wanted to. To have people want to be in my company for a laugh. To have people want to be with me or be away from me for any reason apart from money. I'm not saying I'm working-class, or any class. I just wanted to start at the bottom, like everyone else. Live my life and settle in where I fit, not where some fucker chooses to put me.

The more time I spend with the others and the more things we do together, the stronger our relationships will become. The one thing that has bonded us all from the very start is the will to make extra cash. I needed to do something that would detach me from my past and make them believe that I'm the same as them.

After the robbery there would be no turning back. We'd be in too deep and my commitment to them could never be questioned. The robbery: bottle, togetherness, eclipsing anything any of us had ever done before. It wouldn't matter how any of us had got to that stage, we'd just be there – together. No looking back.

I'm sure it was Gregg at the door when I was talking to Buckley. What if he tried to fuck everything up for me, without giving me a chance? If he was on the level why didn't he stay in the flat and confront me straight away? There's only one reason and that's to get the others against me before I'd had a chance to explain.

I raced down the stairs, across the road and into the park. He was always first back from the afternoon jobs. If he had anything to say, let him say it to me first. Why should I be the one to make way? He'll think because he's bigger, a few stone heavier, that I couldn't handle him. I could handle him all right. If it came to that – I could handle him.

Gregg sauntered along the footpath, munching on something in a paper bag. "What the fuck you doing out here?" He cuffed me round the head and we made for the flat.

The others came in and nothing was said.

We went through the plan to get into Jeff's office, then got ready for work.

6

We arrived early for work, clocked in, and made for the smoking room. This was my first night back since the weirdo had been taking photos of me and I was keeping an eye out for him. Maybe he wasn't connected to home. I doubted it, but what if he was just a perv and took a shine to the way I was stacking those tins? Or from the benefits office, mistaken identity? It's possible. Christ, it says something when you hope that a stranger photographing you is a nonce rather than to be connected to home.

We started our shift and I pushed the fresh supplies though the double doors and into the fruit and veg section. After unloading the trolley, I headed back into the warehouse, carried on past the frozen section and stood with my back to the rear wall of the fish, meat and deli counters. To my right was the smoking room and staff room. Jeff's office was straight in front of me. There were cameras pointed at the stored foods and entrance to the delivery yard. I was just about to walk over and try Jeff's door when he stepped out. He pulled the door closed behind him, waved at the security camera and headed out the service yard door.

I returned to the shopfloor, went over to aisle 18 and knelt down next to Gregg. "He doesn't lock it."

"Fucking hell, Spence," he said falling back. "I'd just opened the safe."

I started packing. "Much in?"

"Chocker, obviously."

"I've just been out back next to Jeff's office. He definitely didn't lock his door, just walked straight out."

"What about the cameras?"

"All pointing at the exits and the food. I'll see you at bait-time."

The next couple of hours flew by as I kept a watch on the comings and goings to the warehouse. I reckon midnight would be the best time to rob the place because most of the staff clock off then. We could mingle with them on our way to the secure door and when we came out there'd be hardly anyone around.

Cam knelt down next to me and started babbling on about roast chickens and how they ran out an hour before they did last night and that one old dear was going to put an official complaint in. He was talking so fast I could hardly understand him. I slowed him down by saying things like, *really* and *life on the edge* and *the world of chickens is most fascinating, Mr Brazelle*. When he eventually stopped bombarding me with jumbled sentences, he stood up and said, "Look, I need a word."

I leant back on my honkers. "What about?"

He shifted his weight from foot to foot. "Can we... in private, I mean."

I finished unpacking the tray in front of me.

I ripped open the last tray on the trolley and took my time filling the shelf.

Cam patiently waited.

I'll tell you what I think. It was Cam who overheard my conversation to Buckley. If he hadn't, why come and see me when I might not even remember he'd tried it on? He was going to blackmail me to safeguard his secret.

I led the way to the warehouse.

By the time we reached the service yard door I was seething. He felt too close to my back when I opened the door and I discretely picked up the metal shutter handle and walked out into the warm air.

I spun around, keeping one hand behind my back. "So what's up?"

He pulled his hairnet off and ruffled his hair. "Look, Spence, about the other day."

"What about it?"

He hesitated, then felt for his smokes and offered me one. "I just need to know where I stand. After the acid party. I'll understand if you think I'm disgusting, but I'm through with denying it." He took a massive draw, nervously touching at his face and hair.. His eyes filled up and he turned away and booted the plastic bin.

"You've got nothing to be ashamed of, Cam," I said,

laying the handle down. "Obviously I'm not into it, but it doesn't bother me at all. Straight up, nothing's changed as far as I'm concerned."

He stood with his back to me, hands spread-eagled on the wall.

He composed himself, then sat on the metal step and had another smoke.

I told him we were mates, no matter what.

He relaxed and confided in me some more, mostly about back home in South Africa and how he thought one of his brothers was gay too. And that his best mate had been a lesbian, which was a great smokescreen for them both. His father, he said, would probably kill himself rather than live with the shame. He said I was the first straight person he had tried to tap up – and I would be the last.

I promised I wouldn't tell anyone, even in jest.

We had another smoke.

I told him that I fancied Amber.

"You don't say."

"Is it that obvious?"

"Yip."

"She doesn't fancy me though, does she?"

He shrugged. "Hard to say with Amber, but you two have been real tight since the acid party."

The door creaked open and Gregg's fat face appeared. "What the fuck you doing! We shouldn't be seen together like this! Or even talk to each other in public!"

"Talk about me shitting myself," Cam said, flicking his smoke away and pulling his hairnet on. We went back inside.

Gregg and I casually walked over to Jeff's door, checked both ways and ducked inside.

We could hardly see a thing and I was beginning to think it was a waste of time when Gregg switched the light on. I instinctively crouched down, saying, "What the fuck you doing?"

"Think about it," he said, leaning against the desk. "There's no window, at best someone might see light under the door, but I doubt it. So there's no need to be in the dark, is there?"

"Suppose not."

The office was small, with a desk and filing cabinet, drawing board, and a door in the far corner.

"What's in there?" I asked.

"Boxes of nails and screws and other shite he hoards, and a few power tools."

I sat in the swivel chair and began looking through the paperwork in his in-out tray, then flicked open his desk diary; crafty bugger was picking supplies up at eight-thirty on two mornings and last thing on Friday – nice way to get on flexitime.

"Look at this," Gregg said, pulling a construction drawing from the bottom of the pile. "The CCTV room is next to the manager's office, first on the right as we go in. And the safe room's next door."

We rummaged through the plans and I pulled an electrical drawing out. Written inside the CCTV room were the numbers 4548. Gregg scribbled it on the palm of his hand and we went back out onto the shopfloor.

We finished the shift and resisted talking about our discovery until we were heading through the park towards the flat. We all agreed that the numbers must mean something, but if the doors were opened with a key, then we were no closer to finding a way into the surveillance room.

It was three in the morning. Cam knocked up, Gregg got the beers, and Amber changed into her tracksuit bottoms and sweatshirt.

As the drink and smoke kicked in and we got the customary bang on the floor from Mike downstairs, we threw around some figures on what we could expect to pocket. We didn't know exactly when Securityinc collected, but we guessed every two days. If timed right, the Sunday of a long weekend would be a whopper payout.

"Half a mil," Gregg said, stretching to the ceiling. "Easy."

"A quarter," I said.

"Ten years minimum," Cam said.

Amber had been told that getting trained to work on the tills would be no bother and to ask Aileen on the next shift. We eventually went to bed with more problems to solve. How often did Securityinc call?

Electronic pad or keys? Who cashed up? And who had access to the safe?

7

A week after we had been in Jeff's office, Amber had completed her training and was on till duty. Until she managed to get a look in the back rooms, our escape plan was the only thing we could work on.

To carry the cash across the shopfloor, Gregg came up with the idea of changing into our normal clothes in the safe room and strolling out the main entrance. Far too risky, I said – whether in the secure area or on the shopfloor, being shelf packers was our best cover.

"Agreed," he said. "But all it takes is one person to ask what's in the bags and we're fucked." He stood at the fireplace massaging his temples. "Picture this. Quarter-past-twelve, bags loaded. We check the coast's clear and make a move, yeah?" We nodded. "We've got no chance of making it out."

I frowned. "How do you get that?"

"If we can't make it out," Cam said, "we can't do it."

"Think about it. The front entrance is a no-no, because of the cashiers and cigarette kiosk, so it's got to be the back way, yeah?" I nodded. "We turn right, up aisle 24 and into Beers and Wine – Jason stands there nearly all the time."

He had a point, the security guard stood at the start of Beers and Wine, and Toiletries (alcohol and razors were stolen most often); from there he could see along the crossing aisle, the deli, and the secure area. We either had to pass the security guard and the deli counters to go out the back, or the cashiers to go out the front.

"There's only one route as far as I can see," Amber said, standing up and pointing at the construction drawing. "Out the mirrored door, then we turn right up aisle 24. That way we miss the cashiers and everyone at the bottom of the store. Once we reach the crossover aisle, turn left and go along," she nodded her head counting the aisles, "to aisle 16."

"Why 16?" I asked.

"Because we'll miss the deli counters where at least one supervisor will be and we'll be directly in front of the warehouse doors."

"Sounds good, but getting past Jason's going to be tricky."

"Rather him that the cashiers and supervisors though, Spence."

Gregg was unusually quiet.

"Come on then, what do you think?"

He slowly pushed himself up. "A human wallet," he said, looking well smug. "Spence and me get in and get the coin, yeah?" We nodded. "Inside the bag we have a set of maintenance overalls, same as the ones worn by the call-out company. Matching cap, the works, yeah? I'll slip these on, Spence stuffs as much cash on me as possible, thus lightening the load of the tool bag so it looks less conspicuous."

"Less conspicuous!" Cam scoffed. "Than you in overalls stuffed full of money! This is a wind up, right?"

"Spence goes out first and stays in front until we reach the crossover aisle. If Jason's there, Spence keeps him busy. Same again when we get to the top of 16. Spence checks first, if the coast's clear, we're straight into the warehouse, out the door, along the bottom road, avoiding the camera on Hart Street."

Gregg's imagination and resourcefulness was something I greatly admired, but his plan was ridiculous. We agreed that the safest escape route was up aisle 16, so we needed to distract the security guard, keep an eye out for supervisors and pray for some luck. Fuck's sakes, who were we kidding? Dressing up and distracting security guards – absolute fucking joke. Without a look in the back rooms and a realistic escape plan this was never going to happen.

8

A week passed and there was little we could do until we got more information on the back rooms. Amber was permanently on till duty now, but all she ever saw was the back of her supervisor's head after she had handed over her cash drawer.

But that changed on Thursday night. There had been a cock up with the time sheets and two cashiers were clocking off at twelve and Amber had already cashed up, ready to take her break. All we knew, as the four of us made our way home at three in the morning, was that Amber had been beyond the mirror panelled door.

Gregg was pacing, waiting for Amber to come out of the bathroom.

"I'm sorry," she said, fast-walking. In her haste she had forgotten to put on a sweatshirt and her tits were bursting out the top of her black vest. 36DD? Fuck knows, but they were big and she was bouncing around without any regard for poor old me, paralysed in the chair. When she bent over to take her socks off it fucked me completely and I had to sit forward with my head in my hands.

She quickly glossed her lips before starting. "As I

was saying, two cashiers clocked off at twelve and I'd already cashed up, so Eleanor was in a flap with three cash drawers to carry and no trolley with her. Now get this." We edged forward. "I followed her in carrying two of the boxes and she's cursing like mad at the mix-up by Aileen. On the right is the main office." We all nodded, having been there for our interviews. "She marches ahead, past what must be the camera room and stops at the next door. She puts the box down, puts her glasses on and squints at a black plastic card."

"What kind of card?" I asked.

Amber shrugged. "Just like, say, a credit card. Anyway, she moans about the code being changed too often, then types in a number and I follow her inside. The room was about the size of my room, a bit smaller, everything white, loads of cash boxes and a few trolleys."

"Fucking hell," Gregg said, "if we get Eleanor's card and keys we're as good as in."

"Where was the safe, then?" Cam asked.

"There's a mirrored door to the left. It's in there."

"So what happened next?" I asked.

Amber reached for her drink off the coffee table and I was the lucky recipient of some serious cleavage and I slipped back into a trance.

"Eleanor went into the safe room on her own and I waited. That was it."

She couldn't say for sure if the CCTV room had a keypad, but apart from the main security door, the rest did.

Amber went to her room and returned wearing a blue hooded top. She sat next to me, linking my arm. Cam and Gregg were arguing again and Amber intervened. Gregg went off to his room and we reassured Cam he wouldn't be bullied into anything.

The next stage was to get a copy of Eleanor's keys and the codes. We reckoned that if Eleanor had trouble reading the code today, then it must have just been changed because she was in and out of the secure area hourly. Allowing a couple of day's grace made a Friday the best time to steal the codes. If we were going to do this robbery then it would have to be soon, to capitalise on the information we had gathered. It was all too much for Cam and he made for the toilet.

Amber tucked her feet underneath herself, glossed up and nodded towards the bathroom. "He's going to be no good on the night," she said. "I don't even know if I'll be, my heart's pounding now."

"Tell me about it. Last week was just talk, but we know enough now to make a move." I reached for a smoke and handed Amber one. "How we going to get the keys and codes off Eleanor?"

According to Amber, Eleanor was fond of a drink, so getting her plastered and stealing them was the best plan we could come up with.

"What if she doesn't take her work keys out with her?" I said. "And where does she go drinking? We can't hinge everything on Eleanor going on the piss with her work keys, can we?"

"Pity we hadn't thought of it last week. They reckon she was steaming at Andrea's leaving do, necking on with some bloke in the middle of the dance floor and everything. Had to take the next two days off on the sick."

We came up with an idea, but first we needed to ensure that we could get Eleanor drunk on a given night. Taking the last leaving party as form, we decided to stage another leaving do – Amber's.

"Makes sense," she said, re-lighting the joint. "Eleanor would definitely come."

Cam joined us and we filled him in on the plan. A smile spread across his face. There was only one man for this job and how could he refuse after his "do or die" speeches? Right on cue, he came out of his room wearing old work trousers.

Cam knelt up on the sofa. "Are they work slacks, mate?"

Gregg gave us a twirl, before dropping down and doing some press-ups. He then jogged around the kitchen table and over to us. Without saying a word, he pushed the coffee table to one side and began taking the trousers off.

"Don't tell me this is your effort at pole dancing," I said.

"Without the pole," Amber added.

"And without the dancing," Cam said.

We watched, fascinated, as the pants came off and he turned them inside out to reveal his creation. "The human wallet," he said triumphantly. "I've calculated that this," he pulled handfuls of paper, cut the size of bank notes, from the lining of the trousers and threw them around like confetti, "would be about fifty-G. We could carry a hundred grand between us. Anything over goes in the bag. And that little demonstration of agility lasted ninety seconds – the time it takes from the secure door to the warehouse."

"Someone will notice the bulk, mate," Cam said. "They're always on the look out for thieves, you know that."

"You never noticed," Gregg said, leaning towards him. The blue trousers fell to the floor. "The escape route is planned so we miss Jason *and* the gaffers. I'm in uniform, so they'd have to be sure, Cam, and a minute-and-a-half isn't long."

"P-lease," Amber said, dramatically lifting a hand and turning her head to the side. "Get that covered up, those underpants are gagging."

"Is that a coffee stain on the back?" I asked.

"Ha, fucking ha." He snatched the trousers off the floor and marched off.

"You'll have to wear something a bit cleaner than that when you're in bed with Eleanor!" Cam shouted.

The more I thought about it, the harder I laughed until I was doubled over on the floor.

"With her g-glasses on," Cam cried, gripping my shoulder.

Gregg returned and patiently stood at the fireplace,

but it was no use, every time I looked at him I pictured the pair of them in all their glory, slapping about the bed like a couple of seals.

Eventually we calmed down enough to tell him the plan.

"There's fucking no way on this earth I'm shagging her," he said, pacing, "no fucking way, you bastards."

"We've all got to play our part if it's to work," Cam said, quoting his words.

Gregg soon saw the funny side and the jokes got cruder, until Amber stepped in. "Come on, that's not on, she's someone's mam, you know."

Gregg was soon back on form. "I'll get those keys, Cam, don't you worry about that. But when I do, we do the robbery within three days."

That silenced the room. Organising the leaving do and getting Eleanor there would be no trouble. Gregg would get the keys and codes – at any cost. When he did, we were on.

9

Monday night, three in the morning; as we discussed the possibility of using a trolley to carry the cash across the shopfloor, Cam, two hours later than expected, stormed up the stairs and turned my world upside down. He had spotted the bloke with the ginger beard outside Columbian and followed him to a massage parlour. The bloke came out an hour later with a blonde and they staggered arm-in-arm down the road.

"What happened next?" I asked.

I copped a glance from Gregg.

"I followed them to that B&B on Palmer Street and come straight back here."

Why the fuck couldn't he just disappear, crawl back to whatever perv place he came from? Because that's what the fucker must be, taking photos of lads stacking shelves and going to gay bars and brothels. I just wish he hadn't latched onto me. And why hadn't Buckley rang to put my mind at rest?

Fuck's sakes, if I didn't get a bit of space in my head it was going to blow. I was getting a headache on top of a headache, not a migraine, but a steady throb, feels like a heavy lump of rubber in my head, monotonous beat, each problem stretching it further. BANG! Imagine. Hot rubber stuck to the wall, black lies trickling down and a puddle of hate and bitterness. A wasted life. That is the worst thing anyone can be accused of and what I faced if I went back to Newcastle.

I caught Gregg staring at me again.

"I've fucking told you! I don't know why the fucker was photographing me!"

"Whoa!" Cam said, jumping up.

"Fuck this."

"Spence!" Amber shouted.

I ran down the stairs, out the door and kept on running.

I took the first left, then right.

I ran as fast as I could, frantically looking for a way out.

Who the fuck was this bloke?

A dead end.

Why hadn't Buckley called?

Over a garden wall.

Gregg will be telling them now about the phone call, the sly fucker.

Along a high street.

This bloke is going to fuck it up for me.

Through a park.

Gregg's fucking it up for me right now. Phone call? When? Are you sure? Must have something to do with him. Why didn't he say anything?

My legs packed in just ahead of my lungs. I held onto

the gates in front of me. It was pitch-black. No streetlights for miles. The gates were tall, like those to our house in Newcastle. I slid down and wrapped my arms around my knees and squeezed tight, willing it to go away. Willing it never to have happened. I've been here before – all run out, guts twisting with every breath.

* * *

"Spencer! What's happened?" Margaret bent over and lifted me up by the armpits. "Where's your t-shirt. What's happened?"

I couldn't hold it in any longer and burst out crying. I didn't want to cry in front of her because she'd tell my father, but I couldn't help it. She held my hand and walked me down the drive. I switched sides in case anyone saw me when they came along Mill Lane. When we got inside I ran to my room, closed the door and dived onto the bed, face down. I knelt up and puked onto the floor. I could never show my face again. Never. Everyone was in on it. Even those in my class. But it's not true. Wayne and me, we're the same as them.

I moved into the front window because of the smell. I wasn't cleaning it up. Let him. If I hadn't been kept in every night I could have arranged a meet with loads of people. Even if I couldn't, I would have been there at the start this morning and none of this would have happened. I wished it hadn't happened. Not in front of everyone. And what about school? If I didn't go back all summer it would carry on at school. Forever. If Wayne didn't come back before the end of the holidays I wasn't going back down and I wasn't going back to school either.

How did they know Mam had died? No one had ever said anything before. I should have been there first thing this morning.

I tried not to think about what had happened down the park, but it kept coming back and it made me feel sick so I rolled into a tight ball to make it go away. Sometimes I fell asleep, but always woke up suddenly thinking Wayne was at the fence.

My father had sat in on two classes over the past week. He wanted to know why I was making so little progress and kept on at me to buck my ideas up or it would continue when school started. Today he was home early and I heard him shouting at Mr Blake in the hallway. Straight after, he burst into my room.

"What the hell's going on with you, Spencer!" He pulled his tie loose. My father's grey hair falls to both sides, and when he's mad he runs one hand through it and flicks his head back and looks at the ceiling. "I'm paying a fortune to give you the best education and you can't be bothered to even try!"

Something caught my eye and I looked out of the window. It was Wayne! He was back! He gave me the thumbs up. Yes! Yes! Yes! We'd show them once we got down there! What would they have to say now? It would all be forgotten and we'd get our names up for everything like we were supposed to. John Ellis would have to crawl to be our mate and even then we wouldn't let him.

"Are you listening?" Father grabbed me by the collar and forced me against the window. I had never seen him so mad. He looked down at Wayne. "Scum! You hear me!" He let go of me and stepped back. He straightened his shirt and breathed out slowly. "Now, listen to me, Spencer. I'm not having this. I thought we had a deal. You were heading in the right direction, but now you're going back over. This is because you're distracted. You need to be focused on schoolwork until you're at an acceptable standard." He walked to the door. "You're grounded until I see some results."

"No! Please, Father!" I chased him down the stairs and into the kitchen. "Please, I'll do anything, just let me out tomorrow. I'll do double, just let me out tomorrow. Pl-ease."

He opened a drawer, took out a cigar and sat down at the table.

Arms tight to my sides, I clenched my fists and tried not to cry.

"Go ahead," he said, lighting the cigar, "it'll do you no good. You're grounded until you reach an acceptable standard. If that takes the rest of the holidays, then so be it. Now get to your room."

I ran to my room and jumped onto the bed and punched and punched and punched and punched. I had to go out tomorrow. I just had to. Wayne was back and everything could be put right. I'd stay in forever, but not tomorrow. I had to go out. I had to.

The first few days Wayne came by to see if there was any change. After that he didn't bother. We were into week three of the holidays. I knew I'd never do well enough to get out. This is what he wanted all along, for me to stay in and do schoolwork. Nothing else mattered to him.

One afternoon, Wayne came past with John Ellis and a few other lads and he didn't even wave, just ran straight past. What was he thinking of? I couldn't believe it. What if Wayne became one of them? Turned against me and joined in giving me the bumps? What if they saw Margaret at the window with me? They'd think it was all true! There'd be no way back!

I waited for Wayne to pass on his way back. I'd get his attention and meet him at the fence. I had to tell him today. I couldn't wait any longer, not with John Ellis poisoning him against me. It had to be today. What if he never came back this way? He had to. He had to. It was the quickest way back to his house. I had a chair in the window so I could reach right up and shout out of the window. I had to speak to him today.

I refused to let Margaret in my room. She didn't mind and left my lunch on the landing, but I pushed a set of drawers across the door just in case she forgot. When I heard the door bang against the drawers I thought it was

Margaret, but it was Father, home early again.

"What the…" he shoved the door open and squeezed through. "What the hell's got into… Jesus, Spencer!" He ran towards me and knelt down. "Son, what have you done?" He held my arm and pulled the sheet away. My arm had been really itchy and I didn't realise it was bleeding so much.

"Come on, up you get, let's get this cleaned up. I'm taking you to the doctors."

The next couple of weeks I refused to work with the tutors. Father was furious and threatened to change my school, but I knew he couldn't do that until I was eleven. I hated him so much for grounding me because I hadn't done anything wrong. Some kids at the school had been caught smoking – smoking at nine years old – and they were still allowed out. Wayne had said his dad hadn't heard of anything like it and that we were far too young for extra tuition anyway.

It was a Monday night and I was at the front window. Father's black Mercedes crawled up the drive, followed by a blue car that I'd never seen before. A small woman, official looking, stepped out of the blue car. She had dark straight hair down to her shoulders that curled under at the bottom. She shook father's hand and followed him inside.

A while later, she knocked on my door. "Ok if I come in, Spencer?"

I nodded.

Close up she looked older and *very* official, nothing like Margaret. Father should never have sacked Margaret.

The woman sat on the chair at my writing desk.

"Spencer, my name is Carol Jordan. I'm a child psychoanalyst." She pulled a folder from her bag. "My job is to try and help children when they're having a few problems. It may be with just a little thing, a small worry say, that maybe they can't tell Mum or Dad about. Or it may be something far greater than that."

I stared out of the front window. The tree was full of birds hopping from branch to branch. There had been a lot of blue tits there recently. I put that down to Margaret throwing nuts around the lawn. I liked that about her. I decided to feed them from now on.

Miss Jordan had been talking for ages, "… that you're not eating, or talking for long periods. If it's only because you've been grounded, I can understand that; it's a terrible thing being kept from your friends. Is this all that's bothering you, Spencer?"

She asked me a lot of things, like my daily routine, things I only do once-a-week, once-a-month, ten things I like, ten things I dislike.

"Not necessarily hate, Spencer," she said, when I mentioned Father, "just things that you dislike, or would like to change for the better."

I switched windows. It was about this time when they'd be coming back and I wanted to know who else had joined the gang – hopefully no one.

Miss Jordan got up to leave and thanked me for being so helpful. She shook my hand. "What's happened to your arm?" she asked, touching the bandage.

"I've been to the doctors. It's exma."

"You mean eczema," she said.

I nodded and she walked out.

I heard Father's voice downstairs and tiptoed out onto the landing.

"Mr Hargreaves, it's quite possible, and with further sessions I'd be more assured in my assessment, that Spencer is still coming to terms with the loss of his mother."

"That's ludicrous! His mother's been dead three years. He never even mentions her. All he wants to do is kick about the streets with the no-hopers. My father stopped me when I was his age. I know what it feels like. But he was right, and I thank him for it now."

"I feel the root of his problems is maternal deprivation and, if I'm being honest here, you're not helping matters."

"Me! I'm the only person that gives a damn. I work all the hours to take this family forward, something he'll inherit in later life. Miss Jordan, Spencer will have the world at his feet. I want him well-equipped to deal with it."

"Love and attention is what Spencer needs, not all this regimental teaching. I'm not saying it isn't good for him to have extra tuition, but not at the expense of love and care from you."

"He knows I love him. Jesus, we've only got each other. He's young. He knows I work a lot, always have, but he's the one that'll benefit. He's too young to understand the big picture. What I need to know from you, Miss Jordan, is how to get him out of this slump before the new term starts. Give me a second, I need to take this call."

Ten minutes passed.

"Sorry about that. Where were we?"

"Mr Hargreaves, I have many clients, most of whom don't require home visits. My time is precious to me, as I know yours is to you. Your secretary has cancelled three of our appointments before today, and delayed this one by an hour."

"My apologies."

"What I'm telling you about your son doesn't take much working out. After I spoke to him at length it's clear he dislikes you and blames you for his problems. It's quite probable that he has developed an anxious and avoidant attachment to you, avoiding any contact with you when you do eventually return home. One of the things he told me he would like was a lock on his room door. Why do you think that is?"

"Of course he's got the hump with me. I'm the disciplinarian. He's bound to hate my guts. I hated my father, but by God I was thankful later when I turned out like I did. Spencer will be the same."

"He's got no stability in his life except you, and that

route is being closed off to him, leaving him isolated. He's badly cared for, Mr Hargreaves."

"What? I can't believe I'm actually paying to hear this. Listen to me. He gets only the very best childcare. All nannies are vetted and come from a top-class agency. Believe me, if his work suffers or they don't toe the line, they get shown the door."

"I've no doubt, but that isn't helping Spencer."

"Rubbish. He's a bit down because I wouldn't let him out and he's taken it too far with this non-eating and sitting in the window."

"Losing his mother at such an early age is a stressful life event. Some people can't cope and it can have long-term effects."

"Such as what?"

"The list's endless. Diabetes, heart attacks, anxiety attacks."

"For Christ's sakes he's only eight-years-old! Eight-years-old – pedal bikes and football, that's what his world revolves around."

"What happened to his arm?"

"Yes, well, that's another story. The doctors say it's eczema. Quite common."

"Eczema may or may not be common among kids. What I do know is that when I asked him about certain subjects, such as his friends, or going back to school, he started scratching his arm."

"Yes, that did concern me. It's one of the reasons I pushed for a meeting with you today. One day he refused to let the nanny into his room and when I arrived he was covered in blood. Scratched right through the skin on his arm. That's when this all started, but the doctor put us straight, said it was common."

"Mr Hargreaves. It may have started out as eczema. But Spencer, in my opinion, suffered a panic attack. That's how he didn't know when to stop scratching. Probably couldn't have stopped if he wanted to. Although it is difficult to determine anything in one session, it is my opinion that Spencer is suffering from anaclitic depression, brought on by being badly cared for. Anxiety attacks are a common symptom of this."

Stones scattered off my window and I tiptoed back into my room.

* * *

Palmer Street was lined with tall mature trees down both sides, the roots cracking the footpaths and garden walls. Cars were doubled parked the full length. A couple of street lamps were off. The dark blue front door of number 154 was halfway down. I stepped over the garden wall and made for the side of the house, then waited; there was a street lamp buzzing, water dripping from an overflow and a woman's muffled voice, occasionally high-pitched – had to be the pro Cam had seen him with. The curtain moved and a woman laughed, then shrieked. I pulled myself up onto the sill, leaning heavily on my elbows, and listened: low hum of music and the woman's voice.

A car stopped in the back lane and two lads in white shirts got out and slammed the doors shut. They came round the front, walked past me, then suddenly took to their toes. The taxi waited another five minutes before reversing up the lane. It kerb-crawled the front street before speeding off.

I listened again. No voices, no music, just the overflow dripping.

I went round the back and returned with a brick. I stepped back and hurled the brick through the window and legged it up the street, ducking down behind a car at the top. Lights came on all over the house and a tall bloke in a dark dressing-gown, white legs, ran out into the middle of the road, panicking. A fat woman joined him, then the skinny son. The son went down in the press-up position and shouted – I'd been seen.

Fast as you like, left, right, left, right, onto Darlinghurst Road, easing up into a jog as I reached the park.

I'd been in the park an hour, maybe two, I'm not sure, when Amber came running towards me. She flung her arms around me.

"I was worried sick! I thought you'd gone for good. What'd got into you running off like that?"

She eased back, resting her palms on my chest. She seemed in no hurry to move away. We awkwardly came together, started kissing and stumbled back onto the bench. In seconds my hands were all over her and I was kissing so fast we were completely out of sync. Amber turned her head to the side and we both moved back.

"Is this your way of asking me out?" I asked, searching for her face.

"*My* way!" she tossed her head back, laughing, but wouldn't look at me.

"Jesus!" she said. "I can't believe we just did that!"

"Didn't you want to?"

"Well, yeah…"

I steamed straight in before she had time to think, though showing more composure this time, arms relaxed around her waist, nothing too heavy.

She pushed back again. "What about the others?"

"They'll not be bothered. You must know how much I fancy you, it's been killing me."

She laughed and tossed her hair back again. "I had noticed."

"And that was long before the vest incident."

"Eh?"

"You parading around the flat the other night in a black vest. I only just managed to hold it together."

"Stop it!" she said, playfully slapping me.

We sat back down, close together, but not touching.

"So, is it fair to say that you and I are a little more than best mates now?"

"We'll have to wait until daylight, see if I still fancy you, or if you're a girl's worst nightmare."

"So you do fancy me? You admit that."

"Did I say that? One thing's for sure you're going to have to... Spence!"

"What?" I jumped up, looking myself up and down. "What?"

"Your arm!" Amber sat me down and held my arm up to the moonlight. "What have you done? Look at all the blood."

"It's eczema. I've had it since I was a kid. I've got cream for it. It looks worse than it is."

"It looks painful. I've never noticed it before." She looked at me. "Where have you been all this time?"

I told her what I had done.

Amber wrapped her arms around me and kissed me. "This is you to a tee, going off on one over nothing. You're so passionate Spence, but sometimes you take it *way* too far."

I shook my head.

"What now?" she said. "You're always doing this. If something's worrying you, just come out with it."

"You know I told you about the inheritance?"

"Not this again. You tell me every time you're pissed that you're going to be loaded when you're older. There's no need. It's the here and now that counts. Forget the future. Who knows what's going to happen? Just forget about it."

"Yeah, but it's more than that."

"That's your business, no one else's. Do you think all of us tell everything about ourselves?"

"I suppose not, but this bloke following me. I'm sure

it's something to with my father. And with the robbery coming up it could cause problems."

"You're looking into things too deeply. No one knows about the robbery bar us, and this bloke hasn't been anywhere near us apart from that first day at the flat. He could be anybody. But you always think the worse. I heard you on the phone the other day –"

"When? When I was in my room?"

"Yeah, saying you thought you were being followed. Totally over the top, but that's you."

"Why didn't you say something instead of running off?"

Amber continued examining my arm. "Why do you think? Because you'd think I thought something was off, that you were a member of Newcastle Secret Service. Am I right?"

"I suppose."

"You worry too much what people think." She kept hold of my hand. "By the way, you owe Gregg an apology. Honestly Spence, he didn't know where to put himself, he really didn't. And he hasn't a clue why you keep having a pop at him."

We walked over to the flat hand in hand.

"This feels so weird!" Amber said, attempting to break free.

We went inside.

There was no one in the living room.

Amber steered me into the bathroom and washed the blood off my arm. "You'll have to stop scratching this."

She patted it dry with a towel. "It's half-five you know. I'm wide awake."

"Same here."

I went into my room and rubbed cream into my arm. I felt light-headed, my stomach turning over and over. I couldn't believe she felt the same way. Couldn't believe it.

Something caught my eye and I turned around and smiled. Hanging from a sweeping brush was Gregg's not-so-white Y-fronts.

"That isn't a coffee stain, is it?"

Gregg followed the light through the door. "That's off that fucking snide ruby we conned out of The Royal the other night. I had proper ring sting for two days."

"Look, Gregg, I'm sorry about before. It's this bloke. And shit from home."

"Forget it Spence. I feel on edge myself with Amber handing her notice in. After tomorrow we've only got three days." He bent down and looked at my arm. "What you done there? And where the fuck you been all this time?"

"You'll not believe what I've done."

I followed him out and went into the kitchen.

"What's he done?" Gregg asked Amber.

I came back in with four cans. Cam was knocking up.

"Tell them what you've done, psycho," Amber said.

"I bricked his window."

Gregg's jaw dropped open. "Who? The ginger fucker?"

"You've bricked his window?" Cam asked.

I nodded.

"You fucking nutcase!"

"Did he see you?" Gregg asked.

"Nah, I was off. I had to see what he wanted."

Gregg burst out laughing.

"What?"

"I can't believe you ran off and done that. You're fucking barmy."

Cam stood up and handed me the joint. "Where's your girlfriend, then?"

"Ah, that's right," Gregg said, leaning against the fireplace. "Where's your other half?"

"I'm not coming out!" Amber shouted from the bathroom.

"You'll have to face the music sometime," Cam teased.

"Nearly ate you alive from what we could see."

"Sod off!"

Amber's leaving party was tomorrow night. In four days' time – it was a long weekend. Cam's idea of using a trolley to transport the cash was the final piece of the jigsaw. On the trolley we'd have two good size boxes. Once we had the cash and videotapes, we'd step out and stuff the bags into the boxes, then push off with the trolley.

Gregg returned from his room. "I know we agreed not to gather any information."

"I had nothing to do with this by the way," Cam said, lifting his hands up.

"Fucking turncoat... but an opportunity came my way and I took it."

"Come on then, what you done?"

Gregg dangled a bunch of keys. "Jeff's keys," he lifted a hand. "Before you say anything, he left them in his door. You know how forgetful he is Spence, that's how we got in last time. All I thought was it couldn't do any harm having them. I'll have them copied and dumped in the car park by eight, someone'll hand them in."

"Fair enough," I said. "I would've done the same. Give me a look."

10

Amber was out sharp in the morning before I'd had a chance to talk to her, so I rang her at lunchtime from work. No answer. Two hours later I tried again and it just rang out. I mean, even if she had her phone on silent, surely she would check it. I sent her a text, nothing heavy, just asking if she was ok. Still nothing.

The rest of the day passed slowly and I left work at half-four convinced she'd left her phone in the flat. Christ, I nearly always left mine because the four of us spent so much time together we hardly ever called each other.

Passing through the park I was joined by the stray dog that had been keeping me company on the way to and from work. I sat on a bench and emptied my lunch box out for him and he ate everything in seconds.

There was a note from Gregg saying they'd gone to The Rocks early to meet people who couldn't turn up later and for me to have my phone on in case he needed any help. I settled in the bay window with a beer.

If Amber had gone early, chances were she hadn't been home because The Rocks was on the other side of town. I went to her bedroom door and rang her number. It was in her room. Fuck's sakes. I sat back down at the window and lit up.

If she'd had any second thoughts about us, me being too keen could well spoil things. There's nothing worse than someone being full on, giving you no space. I had it when I was at private school. One lad was right on my case. I had to tell the fucker to do one in the end.

I had one final look out the window and went into Amber's room. The orange curtains were three-quarter drawn, dust rising up through the sunlight as I stepped over the clothes on the floor. The room hadn't been aired and the bed was unmade. Clothes were heaped in a corner next to her wardrobe. I rang her number, opened her bedside drawers and took out the phone. I erased the missed calls and text, locked it, and put it back in the drawer. I stepped over the clothes and rested my hand on the door handle. The staleness had somehow lifted, leaving only Amber's scent.

Amber turned the corner at the top of the park and I scrambled out of the chair, down the stairs and across the street. She spotted me and broke into a jog.

"Am I a girl's worst nightmare, then?" I asked, kissing her.

"You'll do for now."

The park was heaving, so we walked off the footpath towards the lake. Amber was much more assured than last night and we strolled hand-in-hand past people sitting on the grass.

"How come you've made it back so soon?"

"You won't believe that nutter," she said, rolling her eyes. "No sooner had we got in Jacksons and he was all over Eleanor, hand on her backside after the first drink, *total* mad-eye on."

"Never! What happened next? It's only half-seven now."

"He wouldn't leave her side, kept throwing the drink back. She was loving the attention, at one stage she had her hand inside his pants at the back!"

"No!"

"As God's my witness, Spence. By the time we left Jacksons she was in her element. It looked obscene though, she's got to be nearly sixty."

We settled on the grass behind the kid's play area, and Amber lit us both a smoke. She leaned right into me, checking my arm out.

"Thought I best let some air get to it," I said.

"Looks a lot better."

We sat watching the ducks, crowding the jetty looking for scraps. An old man in a red baseball cap was sat on a bench with his grandson feeding them. I thought of Margaret, my old nanny, she would have been well-suited here.

Amber was lying on her back, head in my lap, fidgeting with my hand.

The stray dog was doing its rounds and getting little joy. It worked the benches along the main footpath, before peeling off towards the lake. It saw me and headed straight over.

"Here's someone I want you to meet."

"You're kidding," she said, sitting up and re-doing her ponytail. "I look a right clip, is it Craig from the garage?"

I patted my knee and the black mongrel sat down. "Teatime buddy, this is Amber, my other half."

"Teatime buddy! Isn't he lovely!" She vigorously scratched his chest and ears. "Aren't you lovely, eh?"

"Follows me to work and back on the strength of a guaranteed feed."

"I wonder where he lives?"

"I'm not sure, he heads left when I go through the gates, so probably down the bottom next to the bottle shop, or he's on his own."

Amber insisted on going to the shop to buy the dog a sandwich. The streetlights had come on and the park was emptying by the time we got back. I fed the last few birds that were hanging around and the dog got two sandwiches. Once the sun had dipped behind the last outline of buildings, we made for the flat. The dog was sticking close to my side.

"I hope it's got somewhere to stay," Amber said, looking down over my shoulder. "It could freeze in this weather."

"What weather – it's roasting!"

"Wait a second." The dog went into the first set of bushes and never came out. "Ah. Shall we bring him inside?"

"Are you insane? It's probably riddled with fleas, and what we going to do with it after Sunday?"

"I forgot about that, you're probably right, and it can't come to that much harm in this weather, can it?"

We went inside and Amber switched the ghetto blaster on and squeezed us a glass of wine each from the goon bag, while I knocked up. After a few blasts of the joint we stretched out on the sofa.

Sometime much later, just as I'd won the battle of wills and released the catches on Amber's bra, Gregg shot up the stairs and slapped the landing light on. His face was blazing red, his white shirt creased and stained with drink.

"You owe me big-time," he panted, "fucking big time."

It was half-twelve. The shower went off and he came out, struggling into a brown t-shirt.

"I hear you're in love," I said, passing him a joint.

"Love?" he shook his head. "Ever heard of periontis?"

"Periodontitis you mean," Amber said. "Gum disease, my grandmother had it."

"Granny sounds about right," he said, twisting his face. "Eleanor's bottom set were only fucking false, can you believe it? She laid the fuckers on the bedside table!"

"You've having a laugh," I said. "And you managed

to bone her with her nashers chattering away on the table?"

"I can't listen to this!" Amber said, hands over ears, fast-walking to the bathroom.

"Honestly, she's so fucking saggy, you just wouldn't believe."

I was squirming as he went into detail. "Did you do the business then?"

"Are you for real or what? There was *never ever* going to be any penetration, but I overdid it plying the fucker with treble gins, crazy cow played hard to get when we got back to her place." Amber returned. "Just so you know.'

"Please, nothing graphic. I heard the penetration word and I nearly chucked."

"*No* penetration, for the record. Anyway, she was there in all her glory, fumbling around, then she passed out and I went straight for her bag."

"And?"

Gregg pulled out a piece of paper and bunch of keys. "Oh, yes."

I leapt on him. "Fucking get in! Get in! You fucking nutter!"

"Unbelievable!" Amber screamed, joining in. "Only you!"

"I'll tell you what, though?" Gregg said, peeling us off him and reaching for a smoke. "She'll be off work tomorrow, no doubt about it, but we need to get these keys copied and back to her or she'll be onto me.'

In less than thirty-six hours we'd be on our way to rob Vasey supermarket. I was looking for a way out. I didn't need to do this now. I had Amber. Life couldn't be sweeter. Whatever we stood to make off the robbery, if we managed not to get caught out by some blatant oversight, I already had in the bank. Ok, I wouldn't feel totally comfortable coming right out and telling them all, but Amber knew I had money coming and the rest she'd understand. Gregg would be the one I'd lose. The two of us had become so close planning this, if I walked away from the robbery, I walked away from him.

Just about anything could happen on the night and the more we talked about it the more we freaked each other out. It was one-thirty.

Gregg looked around. "I've just realised, where's Cam?"

"Haven't a clue," I said.

"Could be out with his friend from the Traveller's Rest," Amber said.

Gregg walked over to the window. "On an important night like this? I doubt it."

Gregg switched the light off. "Come here," he said.

Amber and I joined him at the window.

"It's him, isn't it?"

Cam was sat on the first park bench, elbows on knees, smoking.

"His nerves'll be shot to fuck," Gregg mumbled on his way down the stairs.

Half-an-hour passed before they came back in.
"What's up?" I asked
Gregg tossed a newspaper at me. "Inside page."
Amber rushed over to Cam. "What's wrong?"
"I'm out of here tonight, no matter what."

ATTACKED MAN FOUND DEAD IN HIS BED

Mystery surrounds the death of a man found in his bed early this morning. Police today said they were treating the death of the 53-year-old as murder and launched an enquiry as they waited for the results of a post-mortem.

Det Insp Callum Knight of Kings Cross command area said: "Further tests are being carried out and more enquires are being made. Two men were arrested in connection with the enquiry and have been released with no further action. An e-fit of a man seen following the victim home from Oxford Street last night, between the hours 1am and 2am, has been released. The man is between 5–8 and 5-11, blond hair, slim build, wearing jeans and a blue t-shirt. We urge this gentleman to come forward so we can eliminate him from our enquiries."

Officers found the body of the 53-year-old after responding to a disturbance at a bed and breakfast on Palmer Street. The street was sealed off last night and today as police carried out their enquiries. An eyewitness, who did not want to be named, said, "I heard a window smash, looked out and saw a man running up the middle of the road. It was total chaos, people in the street, police everywhere."

Police also want to speak to a taxi driver who dropped two men off in Palmer Street around this time.

Det Con Sean May added, "We know Oxford Street was crowded around this time with night clubbers and that the victim walked home alone. If you have any information or were on Oxford Street or the surrounding area between 12.30am and 2.30am, or recognise the man in the e-fit, please contact us."

The e-fit was a ringer for Cam.

"I'm getting my stuff," he said.

"I was there last night! I've been seen running up the fucking street! That brick could've killed him!"

"Calm down, Spence," Amber said, grabbing my hand. "We still don't know if he had anything to do with us."

"If he didn't before, he fucking does now," I said, pacing. "I bricked his window! I could be guilty of killing the fucker!"

The ginger bloke hadn't come out into the street. Every fucker else was out, but not him. I pictured him lying on his back, brick by his side, blood running down his face, soaking into his beard, eyes bulging, gasping for breath. Fuck! Fuck! Fuck!

"SPENCE!" Amber screamed.

"Spence, come on mate," Gregg was saying, pulling me up off the floor. "Let's just chill out, take it easy."

Amber prised my arm from my side. "Your arm's

bleeding again. You're going OTT. Please, Spence, just calm down. For me?"

The two lads in white shirts, the taxi pulling away in the back lane, and me, the killer, standing in the shadows with my brick. Why did I go there? What could I have sorted even if I'd seen him? Fuck all, that's what, and now look what I've done.

"Says here," Gregg said, showing me the paper. "Top of the next page. That he'd been assaulted and strangled."

I read the words twice.

"Thank fuck for that," I said, taking a walk. "Fuck's sakes, honestly, I thought I'd done him with a brick."

Cam dumped his backpack at the door.

We had a couple of drinks and tried to make sense of it all.

The reality was that we'd been caught up in this man's death. Cam and I had been to Palmer Street last night and could be implicated. Facts could get distorted. The newspaper report had said the victim had walked home alone, which meant the prostitute Cam had seen hadn't come forward, making her the prime suspect, and our first line of defence if we ever got dragged in. We had two choices: go to the police or leave town.

11

My initial reaction was to pack up and fuck off, and whoever wanted to join Amber and me were welcome. By the time I fell asleep, my attitude had changed. A life without Gregg and Cam made me uneasy. Amber and I would be fine all loved up, but these two were my best mates – my only mates.

I considered telling them about my past to get out of doing the robbery, but all the reasons why I hadn't done it before were even stronger now after seeing their reactions to the stalker's death. So how could we keep it all together without giving the robbery a go?

I woke up on the sofa next to Amber. My head was splitting. Cam was sat in the armchair, legs hanging over the side, blowing smoke rings. Amber stirred and went to the bathroom. I made the coffees and poked my head into Gregg's room on the way back – all his stuff was there but he was gone. Cam half opened the curtains and the sunlight cut across the room: cans of lager, dope tray, two full ashtrays, plastic glasses on the floor and two pizza boxes.

Gregg breezed up the stairs, whistling, armed with

McDonalds bags. "Four double cheeseburger meals." He plonked himself down in the armchair and winked at me.

"So," Cam said, wafting a chip at Gregg. "You've been all the way to Liverpool Street and back, and managed not to eat your meal."

"Or," I said, "you sat in and had pancakes and syrup first."

"Or," Amber said. "You had a big breakfast."

"Big breakfast," he said with his mouth full. "I need extra nourishment when I'm stressed."

We finished our breakfasts and passed the smokes around. Gregg handed me the morning paper. "Page five, bottom left."

The follow up story to the murder was brief. The police had arrested a prostitute and she was helping them with their enquiries, and they still wanted people to come forward if they were in the area between 12 and 2.30. I passed the paper around.

"Right," Gregg said, standing up. "There's not a single mention of Cam or you, Spence. Like we said last night, it had to be her, or her pimp, or something to do with her, or she would have come forward straight away, wouldn't she?"

"It's got nothing to do with us and we didn't," Cam said.

"Now, I know we could have done without this before Sunday."

"I'm leaving today," Cam said. "I'm sorry, mate, I

know what this means to you, but I just can't go through with it."

"Couldn't agree more, Cam. You're a liability. If you head out the door now in broad daylight you could get fingered from that e-fit. Citizen's arrest, even."

"Well, cheers for that. So I'm a liability now, and likely to be arrested on sight if I leave the flat? Why don't I just hand myself in straight away and ask for a shorter sentence?"

Gregg reeled off the endless scenarios of how Cam could be captured, including making an arrest himself here in the flat. *The Outlaw Cam Brazelle, Cam Hood Prince of Thieves, Cam The Terrible, Cam Kimble – The Fugitive.*

"Fuck right off! You're not taking this seriously!" He was up out of his chair. "I could be arrested! God knows what they class as evidence!"

"Just chill," Gregg said, all hands. "Sit down and listen to what I've got to say."

Cam sat back down.

Gregg stared at me. "You know we've got everything we need to pull this off."

"Yeah, but don't forget, the longer we hang around here the more risky it'll be."

"Tonight. Me and you. Nothing heavy, just slip into work, nice and easy; if it feels right we'll give it a shot. If the vibe's wrong we head back, meet these two, and we're on the next bus out of here."

This was the way out for us all. Into the back rooms,

see how far we get, slightest sign of bother, we leave it alone, saving face by at least attempting it. At worst, we get caught in the back rooms and get a warning. Tomorrow, a fresh start and I'll tell them about home, and we'll piss ourselves laughing that we tried to rob Vaseys when we didn't need to. I'll sell the house and business, and we'll pool the money and head up the gold coast in style, partying in Airlie Beach, diving the barrier reef, Thailand, Ibiza, the lot.

Gregg was following me around the flat. "Nothing hard and fast, Spence. Just go to work tonight, see how the land lies, any grief and we're out of there. That's all I'm asking."

"We can't leave until dark anyway, can we?" I asked Amber. She shrugged.

Gregg was in front of me, palms open. "What do you say?"

"Wouldn't hurt to see how it lies just for an hour."

12

I went over to the garage and told Craig I was leaving, and he was genuinely gutted, asking me to do one last bumper day on the petrol con. Problem was, the roadworks were still on and the traffic was hardly moving. The first one we did conked out only fifty yards away and Craig had no room to get in front of her and it caused havoc. We ended up towing the miserable cow away for free.

I grafted hard for the rest of the afternoon. Seemed only right, and I enjoyed it. Come four o'clock I was fully focused on the night ahead. If we did manage to get in and rob the place, Gregg and I would have to go back and work as normal the next day to avoid suspicion. This hadn't been mentioned in the morning, which is why I thought we were acting this out to keep the bravado going that we'd done our best. We weren't all mouth.

I finished work and promised to keep in touch with Craig, agreeing to meet up in Airlie Beach soon. I zigzagged through the traffic and caught a train at Wynyard and got off a stop later at Circular Quay. I bought a fanta orange and stood at the railings next to the ferry terminals, looking out over the harbour at the bridge and opera house. I love it here. I had my girl, my two mates and a job. Where the fuck were we going to go after tonight?

Amber finished work at four every day and arrived home no sooner that half-five. I can't remember her ever getting back before then. She gets on the train at North Sydney and gets off five stops later at Kings Cross. It takes fifteen minutes, tops. What does she do for an hour-and-fifteen every night? Not just occasionally, every night? We'd been on the text all afternoon and come to think of it a few of her later texts were a bit short – not abrupt as such and always with a treble kiss – but, if you looked at them carefully, definitely hurried. It was too late to go over now.

Walking through the park, I was joined by the stray dog. When he'd finished eating the sandwich I'd given him, he stretched out over my feet. I sat for a while, sun warming my face. I watched the old man with the panama, hunched over, shuffling along. I found his battle to get to the end of the footpath each night therapeutic.

Something's bothering me and I'm fucked if I know what. Something right in front of me, a blatant piss-take, and I can't see it. It's not Amber. Can't be. She loves me as much as I do her. No doubt.

Could be Cam. The fucker isn't coming tonight. Why is that? He'll be happy to split the money when we leave, so why not come tonight? Two reasons I reckon. One, because he's shitting it about the police, and, two, he knows something about the stalker that we don't. I'll tell you what, if Cam wanted to, after tonight, he could fuck the lot of us over big time. He'd know about the robbery and be able to place me at the scene with the stalker. And what about the time he pulled me aside to talk about him being bent? I'm fucking sure something was off, I could feel it; the fucker was too close for comfort. I'm not saying he's going to go to the police but, if they gave him a tug, he could escape with a warning while we get done properly.

Fuck knows. Maybe I'm just getting edgy because we're leaving town. If I had things my way I would stay. I'd buy a place here and chill right out.

I took a slow walk towards the flat and promised myself I'd be back on Bondi Beach for Christmas day with Amber. I reached the gates and turned to say goodbye to the dog but he'd taken off chasing another dog.

13

Gregg and I marched to work in silence, the bright green Vasey sign bearing down on us as we walked through the doors and went our separate ways to start the shift. With only a couple of hours to go, I was watching the staff and customers, and looking for a reason to back out.

23.20hrs
Gregg knelt down beside me. "How d'you feel?"
"Calm as you like."
"Guess who's still off?"
"Your bird?"
Eleanor's absence was a bonus, but we needed to find out which key colleague would be standing in for her. Gregg squeezed my shoulder and went back to his aisle. Any excuse would do to call it off, but everything felt right.

0.00hrs
I pushed the empty trolley back through the stream of departing staff and into the warehouse. I checked for the holdalls before taking the next one.

Cam's porcelain white face appeared alongside me. "You all right, Spence?"

My heart started racing; he had dug well deep to get himself here. I mouthed "Keep your eye on Jason", and barged through the doors, along the top aisle and down 23. I passed the crossover as the security guard wandered up 25. Gregg and I came together and he steered the trolley against the security door and bent down for the bags. He opened the door and stepped inside. I checked over my shoulder, pushed the trolley forward and followed him in. We stared back through the mirrored glass: Amber talking to the cashier nearest to us and Cam on the corner of 17.

We pulled our gloves on and crept along the corridor to the CCTV room. Gregg punched in the code and the green light came on. I gripped the handle, sensing someone was on the other side. Gregg pushed past me and I shut the door behind us. "Snap out of it, Spence," he hissed.

00.11

To our left and right there were shelves at head height stacked with papers; on the back wall a grey metal cabinet; right of that a desk with a joystick and a bank of screens, each split into six. The air conditioning unit hummed away as I stared at the door handle, waiting for it to turn. Gregg took Jeff's keys and started on the cabinet. It opened at the fourth attempt. I bent down and ejected the tapes from the three video recorders and stuffed them into the bag. Gregg locked it. We checked around the room to see if there was anything else to take. There was another desk with a steel cabinet beneath it. Gregg tried three keys before I dragged him up.

00.15

Sweat running down our faces, palms itching inside the plastic gloves, Gregg gently turned the door handle, easing it open. The draught blew in the sound of voices. I placed my hand over Gregg's and shut the door. There was nowhere to hide. If they opened the door we were fucked. My guess was a key colleague cashing up because Eleanor, in all the time we had been watching the door, had never cashed up before twelve forty-five.

Gregg tapped his watch – five minutes had passed. He tried the door again and the coast was clear.

00.20

We were six minutes behind schedule when we reached the cash room door. The first code was rejected, the red light flashing like a strobe. The next code triggered the holy green and we were in. The room was tiny, white walls, stack of grey cash boxes, four cashier's trolleys and a door to the left with a one-way glass window. Gregg punched in the code and it opened first time.

00.22

In front of us there were two grey safes, each double

the size of a filing cabinet, with a wheel, a keyhole and a silver keypad. On a table to the left, there were two trays of paperwork, five or six electronic scales and piles of plastic moneybags with Securityinc blazed across them in blue. Underneath, there was another metal container. Gregg tried Eleanor's long key in the first safe and shook his head.

"Try the code first."

He input the last code then tried the key; it turned.

I rushed to the door and checked out of the window.

Gregg was struggling to open the safe and let go of the wheel. "It's no use, Spence, it won't budge."

"Forget it, let's be away before someone comes in. We're fucking bang to rights here."

Gregg lunged at the wheel and pulled with everything he had. I shouldered him aside and tried the other way. Two clunks and the door swung open. The safe was partitioned off with shelves, sand coloured clothbags on the bottom and middle, plastic Securityinc bags on the top. Gregg ripped open a Securityinc bag and showed me – packed solid with notes, *$1000* written on the purple wraps. "Come on then!"

I shoved him forward and he stuffed the plastic bags into the holdall. I went to the other safe and tried the three steps: clunk, clunk. The top two shelves were full of Securityinc bags.

"Just the s-securi bags," Gregg stuttered.

Like a psycho on supermarket sweep, I filled the bag in seconds, topping it off with cloth cash bags.

00.31

I looked through the window and it was all clear. As I turned back I froze. In the far corner a camera was directed at the safes. "Fuck!"

The screen in the CCTV room hadn't shown the safes, so there had to be a separate monitor and recorder. Gregg pulled at the metal container under the table, fumbling keys into the lock, but couldn't open it.

I knew it. I fucking knew it. How the fuck could we not see that camera. Even if we'd seen it we would still have been fucked. Two shelf-packers creeping into the safe room, what excuse could we give? Fucking none. Other than that we were trying to rob the place. Attempted robbery, conspiracy to rob and fuck knows what else adds up to years behind bars.

We sat, backs to the wall, listening to the rumbling air con unit. We had been in the safe room for fourteen minutes, but it felt like hours. I crawled forward, lay on my belly and listened to the metal container.

"This isn't it," I said, clambering to my feet, "Come on!"

00.36

We moved swiftly through the cash room and corridor, stopping at the CCTV door. Gregg opened it at the second attempt and we went inside.

"Under the desk," I said.

"This is it, it's buzzing like fuck."

He tried Jeff's and Eleanor's keys, but couldn't open

it. I took them from him and slowly worked my way through both sets. The cabinet sprung open. Inside was a single screen split in two, showing the cash room and the safe room. I ejected the tape and locked it shut.

00.41

We had been in the backrooms for thirty minutes – twenty longer than planned. Aileen and the key colleagues would be cashing up. If we left now, we could walk straight into a supervisor, cashier or the security guard. We sat watching the screens and the door handle. Five texts came through from Cam wanting to know what was wrong.

Another seven minutes passed and we checked the door again: doors opening and closing and voices. Unless they discovered the cash missing, then it was unlikely that anyone would come into the CCTV room. But still, sitting in plastic gloves, sweat pouring out of us with two sports bags full of cash, we were hardly chilled.

Gregg elbowed me and we leant towards the bottom left-hand screen. It was Cam, standing on the corner of 17 looking well suss. We rolled over silently laughing as he minced off towards the toilets.

00.54

We crept along the corridor to the secure door. There were no customers going through the checkout and Cam was back at 17.

I went out first and pulled the trolley towards the door. Gregg packed the bags into the empty boxes and we made for the warehouse. The security guard nodded as we travelled along the crossover, before turning up 16, onto the top aisle and through the warehouse doors. Cam appeared alongside and helped steer the trolley to its resting place. Aileen was standing outside the staffroom, having a row with a key colleague. Gregg pulled the two bags out and I hoisted one over my shoulder and the three of us walked out of the service yard door.

I dropped the bag at the top of the landing and caught Amber in my arms.

"What took you so long! You should have been back ages ago! I was worried sick."

"You'll not believe what happened," I said.

"Straight in," Gregg said. "Can't believe it."

"Straight in. I swear to God."

Cam was stood at the window. "We've got to get out of here."

Amber searched our faces. "Well then," she said, settling on mine.

"Lift that."

She did.

"Loaded," Gregg muttered, walking away. "Loaded. Yeah, loaded. Look, Spence?"

I lifted my head.

"What the fuck we going to do?"

"What do you mean?"

"I wasn't... I mean..."

"Look," Cam said, lifting his backpack. "I don't care about the money. The last bus leaves in ten minutes and I'm on it."

"If we do one," I said. "They'll be straight onto us for this. You know that."

"Fuck it," Gregg said, grabbing his bags. "Let's be away. If we're miles away, what the fuck can they do?"

There was no chance of us facing the music tomorrow and getting away with it. Even if we could, they'd go after Cam because he'd be the only one that had left on the night of the robbery and when they caught him, he'd fold and we'd all be fucked.

I stepped out into the rain, posted the keys and hurried to catch up with the others. We turned the corner and Gregg ran ahead and caught the driver. Breathing heavily and brushing the rain off, we took our seats.

The driver got off to take a piss and my heart started hammering. I could hear sirens. We looked at each other and I was all for legging it when he got back on.

I checked behind us, still nothing. Just as he started to pull away, something caught my eye. Sat on the pavement staring up at me was the stray dog from the park. He was soaking.

"Let me up," I said to Amber.

"Spence!" Gregg shouted. "What the fuck?"

"Two seconds, mate," I said. "I'm bursting."

"Haven't got time to wait, son."

I jumped off and the driver slowly pulled away.

I jogged into the toilet block, knelt down and wrapped the dog in my sweatshirt. I ran out and chased the bus and caught up at the car park exit and jumped on.

Part 2

14

After counting the cash in a Securityinc bag, Gregg estimated that we had over six-hundred grand. We should be bricking it big time, but we were fucking giddy being on the run. Stars of a top-drawer movie. *Reservoir dogs, Heat, The Vasey Gang.* Why the fuck not? We'd just robbed a top supermarket of all its takings. Best thing I'd ever done, this. No doubt. I know I wanted out early on, but last night and now the buzz, it's unbelievable. I swear I feel like I've just dropped from another fucking planet.

The plan was to stay on the overnight bus until we reached Byron Bay, but after seven hours the driver spotted the dog and kicked us off at Port Macquarie. We sent Amber and Cam to buy a car at the lot we'd seen on the way in. Gregg and I sat outside Café Coluzzi on the corner of Pacific and Clarence, shades on, drinking cappuccinos in the morning sun.

We needed a safe place to store the cash that couldn't be traced back to us. Gregg refused to use a safety deposit box: too many cameras, too difficult to get back out. We scanned the local directory and rang three storage companies, the closest was The Carry Gentle Cargo Company in Kempsey. They had 24-hour security and access, and a room the size of a closet cost $95 per month.

A burgundy Toyota Camry pulled up to the kerb. Gregg shook his head and reached for the bags.

"4x4 is what I said, nugget. What the fuck's this?"

Cam argued that paying any more than three grand in cash for a car would look suss. Gregg snatched the keys and jumped into the driver's seat. Two miles down the road we pulled off into some woods and had ourselves a fire. The holdalls, cash bags, gloves, videotapes, clothes and shoes. Everything. Cam was flapping at all the smoke blowing back onto the road, but we waited until there were only ashes left.

We followed the directions to an industrial estate on the outskirts of Kempsey, and Amber walked ahead with the backpack to hire a locker. Gregg thought the Securityinc bags might have slow releasing ink, so we decided not to take any of the robbery money with us until we knew for sure it wasn't traceable.

Twenty minutes later Amber returned.

"Absolute doddle," she said, getting into the car. "He photocopied my passport and I filled the form in and paid two months up front."

"How big was the room?" Gregg asked. "No way of anyone getting in?"

"About the size of a school locker. Cameras everywhere, and who's going to try and steal a trampy backpack?"

"True, true," I said. "No questions on what was inside?"

She shook her head.

"Fucking yes!" Gregg said, punching the air. "I thought we were never going to get shot of it.'

We stopped at the next services and waited on the corner while Amber filled up. Cam went on foot patrol and returned brandishing a copy of the *Sydney Star*. "Check this out," he said, holding it up. "Ideal place, my friends. It will be a rocking and a rolling for sure."

"Gay festival?" Gregg said. "You're having a laugh."

"You never heard of Fat Tuesday? It's huge! It's not just gays, there'll be hoards of chicks there, mate. Anyone who's anyone will be there this weekend. Here, look who's on, The Killers, Rogue Traders, Kasey Chambers. It's big time, mate. Believe it."

"Who the fuck are Rogue Traders?"

"They sang that *Voodoo Child*, didn't they?" I said.

"A *gay* festival? Definitely not. We need to go to ground until we know what's happening."

"He could be onto something," I said. "We could disappear at a festival, especially one as big as this."

"You heard of it before?"

I nodded. "They reckon it's been going longer than

the Sydney Mardi Gras. It's meant to be jumping."

Cam showed Amber the advert. "What do you think?"

"Ah! Yes! It's meant to be unreal!"

Three against one.

15

Fat Tuesday was held right on the coast between Nambucca Heads and Coffs Harbour at a town called Marasa Bay. Cam rang ahead and there was camping space left, so we stopped off and bought all the essentials.

About a mile out we hit traffic. It was scorching, everyone hanging out their car windows and sounding their horns. Fireworks exploded in the clear blue sky ahead and a massive beachball was being passed back along the traffic jam.

There was a bright yellow Holden Ute in front of us, and one passenger, stood at the cab, was wearing a purple-feathered headdress. The queer fucker turned around and saluted the car behind us and I swear you've seen nothing like the tool trying to escape out the bottom of his purple lycra shorts. Fuck me, he had to be half horse. Had to be. Amber craned her neck to get a look, but he'd turned back around.

A tall black bloke, middle-aged, in white leather hot pants, white wellies and a brown sheepskin waistcoat, jogged down the hard shoulder, followed by a fat lad, skipping along in black leather pants, bare-chested and pierced to fuck.

Cam went over and talked to a few lads that had gathered next to the railings. Amber and I got out and had a smoke.

"What do you reckon?" Cam said, showing us a Zorro mask. "How could anyone find us dressed in these?"

Gregg was doing his nut because the car in front had moved forward an inch. "If any of these fucking weirdoes come near me," he said, "I'll go straight for them. No questions asked."

"You've got to be the most homophobic person I've ever met," Cam said.

"Am I fuck."

"Yeah, you are."

Gregg pointed at a lad dressed as a Charleston Girl, trotting between cars. "Look at that. What the fuck's that all about? Is that what you're into? Dressing up in birds' clothes and wearing makeup?"

"Might be."

Further ahead, everyone was out of their cars hanging over the railings, jumping around.

"Look at that!" Amber shouted.

From the flyover we were on to the sea was about two miles, and every square foot was covered in people partying. Marasa centre was kidney-shaped with a road running right round it. Bikers, a brass band and a farm trailer – with what looked like midgets or kids in cartoon costumes – led the march. The streets around the monument and park were lined with palm trees. Food trailers puffing out smoke were on every corner. Right below us there were old stone buildings, probably the town hall or courthouse.

The traffic started moving, the road swept inland and we were directed into a field to park. We got our bags and tents, and followed the crowd towards the farmhouse. The ten-minute walk in the heat nearly brought us to our knees, but we perked right up when we turned past the building – thousands of tents as far as you could see and everyone was partying. The farmhand took $12 off us, opened the metal cattle gate and let us through.

There was a straw track running right through the middle of the field with revellers heading along it towards a stone arch.

We reached our spot, which was four back from the track. Cam wanted to leave the tents until later, but people were following right behind us and we needed to get set up or we'd lose our place and the gear would probably get nicked. Cam made for the port-a-loos at the far end and Gregg and I started on the tents. Amber gave Teatime some water and food.

Once we had the tents up and gear in, I wandered onto the track and had a good look around. From the farmhouse to the main road was packed solid with tents. Attendants or security guards wearing luminous bibs were posted around the field and at the toilet block, and a few were on the move checking on the campers. Just along from us, there was a dispute going on between an attendant and a jumped-up hippy because he'd pitched his tent too close to his mates and they had a fire going in the middle. Two girls, nude from the waist up and painted green, came skipping towards me. They were wearing orange fishnet stockings with black knickers, and red beads down to their thighs.

Cam leant on my shoulder. "We going to get in amongst it or what?"

Gregg joined us on the track. "I'm knackered after driving. I might just doss here for a while."

"Are you for real?" I said. "Have you not seen the birds heading in there? Fuck's sakes, I thought you wanted your leg over?"

"I'm only joking about the blokes," Cam said. "There'll be more straight people here than gay."

Gregg was in the same clothes we had changed into at Kempsey and looked dishevelled. His shoulders were slumped and his eyes black and sunken.

"I'm going to ring Stevey at the Travellers. See if he's heard anything."

"What if he has?" I said, taking hold of his arm. "What difference does it make now? The longer we stay away from the law, the less lightly it is they can pin anything on us. And the best place to hide tonight is in there, dressed as the four Zorros."

We pulled our masks on and started for the stone archway. The security guard walking the queue stopped at us. "This yours?" I nodded. "It's no fun in there for a dog, mate, he'll have to stay behind."

We took Teatime back and opened the tent door.

"I should stay with him, he'll be confused," Amber said. "What happens if he panics and gets lost?"

"He'll be sound. He knows we'll be back."

We joined the queue and paid our entry fee.

Everybody was desperate to get through the stone archway and out into the daylight and chaos, and I was constantly being nudged in the back. The pounding music, the screaming crowd, the fumes, and the fear of being trampled on, left me short of breath. If we bunched up any more I'd be lifted off my feet and crushed. Why the fuck did they let people through the tunnel at a faster rate than they were letting them out? Fuck's sakes.

We handed our tickets in and stepped out onto the road, and were immediately barged down the street by lunatics waving flags and trying to keep up with the procession. I kept hold of Amber's hand and staggered up a grass embankment to safety. Right next to us a bunch of Rastas were flat out on the tom toms and dustbin lids. I could hardly see anything for all the flags being waved.

The procession disappeared down the bank with many of the crowd following. Gregg and Cam were holed up on the other side of the road next to a food trailer. We weaved through the crowd towards them.

"Have you ever seen anything like this?" Cam said, checking the programme.

"You'll have to speak up," I replied, cupping my ear. "I'm tone deaf from Bob Marley's crew over there."

"Space coming free!" Amber shouted, pointing towards the monument.

We jogged down East Road Boulevard, dodging between trees and leapt onto the small triangle of grass vacated by four cavalry soldiers.

The park was split into quadrants by paving stone footpaths leading to the monument. The monument was of some hero on horseback, and the steps leading up to it were prime seating because you could see down the bank where the official marches carried on. We were on the edge and well shaded by the trees that lined all three sides of the park. I felt much more relaxed here, everyone just chilling out, into their own thing.

Monument Boulevard, on the opposite side to us, was much wider than East Road and Riverside Boulevards, with stalls down one side, punters down the middle and street performers jockeying for supremacy on the other side. I watched a clown follow a family from top to bottom mimicking the father's every move and expecting payment for his efforts. The father was a big bloke with a grey crewcut, his son and daughter both lanky and in their early-teens; he looked like he'd arrived at the wrong festival and was eager to be away. Red-faced, he eventually turned on the clown and the performer scuttled away into the crowd.

There were plenty of people smoking joints, just hiding them when the police passed, so Cam knocked up between his legs and we kept watch. I was fascinated with the man sat along from us. He was in green army uniform, wearing a white John McEnroe headband and sat in a canoe with a cooler full of beer, playing the air guitar. He never spoke to anyone, just merrily strummed away on his imaginary cords. I watched him for a good twenty minutes and I swear he never looked up. I mean, he had to be on acid or some other hallucinogenic drug. Had to be. Not unless he was a proper nut.

After we read the Fat Tuesday programme, Cam filled us in on gay festivals, and how expressing yourself and being free was what it was all about. Apparently, everyone taking the festival seriously had something to say, whether it be a protest or to celebrate, or just to show the world how warped they could be. Personally, looking at some of the fuckers, I reckon they just dress to shock without having any real meaning. Take that one walking past dressed as a Zulu. Honestly, you'd think he'd just walked straight off the battlefield. It wouldn't surprise me to see Michael Cain in hot pursuit. Now how the fuck can that mean anything?

"Get a load of this," Gregg said. "Some serious fucking issues or what?"

An elderly woman, in her sixties, on an ancient bike with front basket, wearing a scruffy wedding dress, came bombing down the road. She was up off the seat giving it big licks, flashing her yellow teeth at us as she went down the hill. Two lads on mountain bikes followed, both wearing cropped fur coats, knickers and suspenders, bras, green curly wigs and beads around their necks. A group of middle-aged men and women in straw hats and black cloaks wandered down behind them. There was unrest in the park and people started making their way up onto East Road.

"Here," Cam said, showing me the programme. "Another parade's starting."

It was nearly half two, so it had to be The Tractor Boys next. We went up onto the boulevard, then onto the side of East Road, which was lined with police and stewards, and cordoned off with waist high red cones and rope. There were two police on horseback making their way through the crowd from the town square towards us, gently breaking them up. We were five from the front, pushing and shoving, trying to look up the street. Air horns sounded and the tail-end of the unofficial marchers cleared the way, leaving the road empty.

Suddenly it felt like the whole town was shuddering under the roar of engines. It went right through me and I jumped up to see what was coming. Harley Davidsons, Nortons and Triumphs rounded the corner in a ten-wide convoy, a skull and crossbones Rockers banner held aloft. The crowd were going crazy and Amber and I were doing the pogo to see over the mass of fluttering flags. A stars-and-bars tractor followed, pulling a colossal statue of a Greek God drinking from a gold chalice. The men riding the trailer were all decked out in black leather pants and waistcoats, bare-chested and wearing sky blue bandanas. The women were in shorts and leather-studded bras and cat woman masks, cracking whips at the crowd.

The bikers started passing us and we burrowed our way forward. Up close, they looked real mean: black potty helmets, mirrored aviator sunglasses, black and grey beards, silver rings covering their knuckles as they revved their engines and looked solemnly ahead. There was a huge three-wheeled bike in the middle, royal blue with yellow flames down the side, and the monster driving it must have been twenty-five stone. He had a long grey ponytail and was wearing the same sky blue bandanna as those on the trailer. The bird riding sidesaddle was a blonde stunner.

As the trailer pulled alongside us, cowgirls in white suede waistcoats, ten-gallon hats, knickers and suspenders, and knee-high black boots surrounded us, *The Dirty Dozen* stamped on their backs.

"Throw me something, mister!" one yelled, pushing past me. The fat biker hanging over the trailer shook his head. The brunette elbowed herself some more space and ripped open her waistcoat, releasing a whopping pair of tits; thrusting her shoulder blades back, she proudly offered them up to the biker, who immediately threw her a skull and crossbones plastic mug. The cowgirl was ushered to the front and wine pumped direct into her mouth from an old fashioned hydrant, and the fat biker leant down and kissed her, all tongues, copping a good feel of her tits as he did.

The resulting stampede of topless gunslingers sent us flying and just before I hit the deck I managed to grab the back of someone's jacket and pull myself up as the crazy fuckers surged down the bank taking me with them.

Turning against the tide, I desperately searched for Amber, but it was impossible to stand still. We bottlenecked at the park entrance and I forced my way towards the town square and out into the thinning crowd.

I ran back to where I'd last seen Amber, frantically trying to find her.

Then I saw the paramedics running across the road with a stretcher. I sprinted towards them, smashing people out the way, images of thousands of boots relentlessly trampling her face into the road. The police were stopping anyone getting near, but I barged past, then sharply turned away when I saw the old woman in the filthy wedding dress being given oxygen. I lifted my hands up, apologising as I walked away.

I jogged back to where I had lost her, and there she was, standing on the corner no more than ten-feet away. A well-built kid was standing in front of her, protective arm stretched out touching the wall.

"Thanks, thanks, honestly I'm fine," Amber was

saying, trying to get past his arm.

I knocked his arm away and grabbed her. "You all right?"

"Spence!" She lept into my arms.

I turned around, keeping hold of her hand.

"Thanks again," she said to the lad.

He was about the size of Gregg, maybe a bit taller and stockier, black hair jelled up in a spike, big fat slavery lips. He was in dark jeans and a red basketball vest, sporting a Maori tattoo from shoulder to elbow.

"No worries," he said, bending down and kissing her on the cheek. As he straightened up his hand slowly fell from her side onto her arse. "You know where I'm staying if you want to call over."

"You fucking what?" I darted straight for him, fists clenched by my side.

"Take it easy, Big Man," he said, hands up. "I take it Amber's not your sister?"

I didn't answer, just stared him out. He slapped me on the shoulder hard enough to lift my foot off the floor. "No offence, mate. You can't blame a guy for trying, can you?"

He winked at Amber and walked away, dragging his feet, nonchalantly checking over his shoulder. I watched the fucker until he joined his pals outside a bar.

We walked down onto East Road Boulevard, keeping an eye out for Cam and Gregg. The park was packed but there was no sign of them.

"Shall we go for a drink?" Amber said. "Them two

could be anywhere."

I shrugged.

Amber steered me past the town square, across Church Street and into the dark alleys of Abbotsvale. The first pub we came to was The Trinity. We took a seat outside under the yellow parasols and ordered two beers and sat in silence.

I wasn't thinking about the arsehole. I was thinking about Amber and what the fuck she got up to in the hour after work every night. Every night. A regular thing going on, which she told no one about. And how the fuck did that kid get her name so quickly?

"Let me guess," Amber said, sipping her beer. "It's my fault for letting him pull me off the floor and saving me from certain death. Then I flirted outrageously with him and gave him my name and number?"

"He got your number as well, did he?"

She pushed her stool away and came and sat on my knee and gave me a kiss. "Can I just say, I love you for it, Spencer Hargreaves. Absolutely... love... you..."

"Now that's more like it!" the barman squealed, coming towards us. He was wearing a white t-shirt and black jeans with a black and gold *Moet & Chandon* piny. He was about five-seven, gaunt, with a black skinhead. He gently placed two purple, green and gold shot glasses on the table. "On the house."

"Nice one," I said, quickly averting my eyes from his when I saw the green eye shadow.

"Can I just ask you," Amber said, holding the shot

glass up. "Why is everything at this festival purple, green and gold?"

He spelled it out on his fingers, "Justice, Faith and Power. Tell me this isn't your first Fat Tuesday?" We nodded. "Dominic!"

A short bald chef, with a couple of day's growth, duck-walked towards us. On reaching our table, he dabbed at his sweaty face and with a heavy foreign accent said: "They refuse my shots?"

"Mardi Gras virgins."

"No!" Shock-horror.

They both pulled up a chair.

Amber coughed after downing the shot. "Wrong way," she spluttered.

"First timers," the chef mused. "What do you think?"

"Unbelievable," Amber said. "Where does everybody get their ideas from?"

"Kyle!" the chef snapped, and the waiter scurried off towards the bar. "This is our big day. People from *all* over the east coast come here to have their say and, of course, they do in the most *flamboyant* way."

"Surely every person in fancydress hasn't got issues?" I said. "I mean, some people, dressed like… like… him!" It was a Zulu with a big fuck-off Afro, carrying a banana stalk, with a lard can tied to his head. "I mean, he must've just watched a few late films last night and knocked that outfit up with whatever he could find in the kitchen this morning."

"Zulu Social Aid, formed in New Orleans *way* back

in the 1900s," he said, nodding, "Ah, ha. African Americans were banned from official marches on Mardi Gras so they formed their own organisation."

The waiter returned with more beers and a bottle of shots.

Amber removed her cap and re-did her ponytail.

"Beautiful hair," the chef cooed. "You *really* should get dressed up for tonight, it's *crazy* after the boat ceremony."

They made us feel so welcome, downing shots, telling us the history of Fat Tuesday and other celebrations around the world that were held on Mardi Gras.

"Fat Tuesday," the chef explained. "Is Mardi Gras in French. And Carnival means removal of the flesh. And *real* carnival people remove their flesh to show who they are on the *inside*. Some people come here not knowing who or what they really are, but often leave with the answers."

The bar was starting to fill up and after a couple of air kisses the chef waddled back inside, leaving us with the bottle of shots.

The Trinity was on the corner of one of the dark alleys and the sun was sprinkling the pavement in front of us through the trees. There was hardly any breeze. Amber and I were playing footsie under the table with people watching. Somewhere in the distance, deep into Abbotsvale, a band was playing reggae music.

Occasionally, heavy drums drowned out their chilled out vibe.

"What do you think's happening back home?" Amber said.

It had been sixteen hours since we'd robbed Vaseys and after stepping through the stone archway into Fat Tuesday, it hadn't crossed my mind.

"They'll be onto us. Got to be, haven't they?" I lit us both a smoke and filled our shot glasses. "But if they can't find us…" I trailed off, watching two blokes, and I mean thickset bikers or builders, one with a trimmed black beard, the other wearing a leather jacket, kissing. They weren't in fancydress, just two regular blokes getting stuck into each other on a Saturday afternoon.

The streets were so narrow in Abbotsvale that the action was always right up close and every second is compulsive viewing.

I looked across at Amber: hair in a loose ponytail, Zorro mask lifted up onto her forehead, tanned arm lying limp on the table, feet stretched out, smoking.

"Are you worried?" I asked her.

She shrugged. "Are you?"

I shook my head.

We drifted back off, people watching.

Amber rocked forward in her chair. "It's weird," she said, criss-crossing her legs with mine. "I feel like I've been here forever. Like last night never even happened."

"I know," I said. "Last night was double heavy, so fast, the adrenaline, but, I don't know, it doesn't feel real now."

We were outsiders here, watching the carnival people, mesmerised at their willingness to show the world their hopes and beliefs, their joys and pains, releasing themselves into this make-believe world where everyone and everything was accepted. Sat here, I realised that us, in our jeans and t-shirts, cards close to our chest, were the strange ones. I was also well pissed off the shots.

The bar and streets around us were emptying as the parade passed by a few blocks away. Amber pulled her stool up and we sat side-by-side, legs stretched out, resting on the metal railings. The two burger-flippers from the food trailers met in the middle of the road for a smoke. We could hear the reggae music again.

Amber was fidgeting with my hand. She dropped her head onto my shoulder. "I shouldn't say this, but I couldn't care if I never saw anyone else again. Cam, Gregg, Dad, Emma, no one. As long as I've got you."

I can't remember how I got started. Everything was mixed up. I wanted to tell her about the money and the company but found myself talking about John Ellis, and how he turned people against me at school. How I knew even then that I wasn't the same as them. They would never have accepted me no matter what I did. I told her what it felt like the first time I found out people talked about me behind my back. How I tried to put it right, face the music, but my father wouldn't let me. I told her how dominant my father was, how well off he was, and that all he ever wanted was his son to be like him. And all I ever wanted was to be like everyone else.

Amber had had it the same when a scandal broke about her mother when she was about eight or nine. She remembered thinking it was impossible, that they had the couples in the street mixed up, but it was true, her mother was having an affair with the bloke across the road. Amber had run home from school that day, desperate for her mother to quash the rumours. She'd opened the front door to complete silence. The kitchen was at the end of a narrow hallway and her father was sat at the table. She ran to him and he hushed her. Amber said she didn't fully understand the situation back then, only that she felt lost.

Amber and Emma were sent to their room when their mother came home. They waited for a big argument, but it didn't come. Neither did their mother to explain the predicament the family was now in. It was their father who gently knocked on the door, sat on the end of her bed and pulled his two girls close, and explained that he would be going away for a while until things settled down.

"It was breaking his heart, Spence. Not only that she had done it, but that she wanted it to continue. He's a proud man and it was humiliating him, but he wouldn't give up on us and he still wanted my mother back. She strung him along, in front of e-everyone..." Amber was crying freely now, "all he ever wanted was to love us and she betrayed him. I've tried to understand it. I have. But she was so heartless wanting it to drag on and hurt him. His face in the kitchen, how could she hurt him like that?"

Amber swore she'd never get married, that it was a sham, and if you loved someone you didn't need a ring, just each other. We were plastered and she was ramming it home about commitment and how she would never be like her mother and if we ever wanted to be with someone else we'd break up first. No lies, no cheating, total honesty with each other.

I told her about switching to a private school at eleven. I left hardly any friends behind at the old school and gained none at the new one. I fell into the 'new money' category and I was way behind academically, which I loved because it pissed my father off big time.

When Amber went to comprehensive school things died down. But back where she lived, there was an attitude towards her and her sister, mostly from the parents.

By the time Amber told me about leaving home to go backpacking, we were slurring every word. Money, the company, why I never told them (she didn't need that explaining she said), why I thought I was being followed, why I hated my father, most of the reasons anyway, how I loved Margaret the nanny. Fuck's sakes, with Amber sitting astride me on the stool, arms around my neck, it all came out in stuttering, sobbing clumps.

Another bottle of shots appeared on the table: *on the house*.

Amber said the same things a hundred times in different words, how she loved me, how she felt safe, how we only needed each other and I was the one for her.

And I believed her. Fuck's sakes, I believed her one hundred percent. Nothing else mattered anymore.

I haven't a clue how long we sat there moulded together, letting it all out, but the drums were drowning the reggae music out again, the carnival people were back on the streets and the bar was full. I leapt up, thrusting my hands under Amber's armpits and lifting her high into the air. I dragged her through the bar, stopping briefly to stuff all the cash I had on me into Kyle's top pocket.

We hit the cobbles running, spinning around, kissing and running for our lives, down Church Street, screaming and shouting, jumping over an old man passed out on the kerb, through the town square, swinging each other around and around, smacking into people, laughing; we didn't give a shit. WE DIDN'T GIVE A SHIT!

We kept on running and jumped the steps into the park, and stumbled forward and fell. The cavalry soldiers we landed on made way for us, and we got stuck into each other like we were in the front room back at the flat. I swear we would have done it there and then if we hadn't ran out of steam.

Amber collapsed on top of me and slid to the side.

There wasn't room to stretch an arm or leg.

The sun was blinding.

Air horns sounded.

A brass band past on the top road, the sound amplifying as it dipped under the flyover.

A DJ was working the crowd over in the square.

We shared a smoke, then fell asleep.

16

I was lying on my back, drifting in and out of consciousness.

I kept feeling for Amber, squeezing her hand.

I tried not to think about my father, but he kept on coming. I hoped he could see me now, see how happy I was, see that I was my own person, see that everything he had done to try and make me be like him, had failed; see how wrong he was.

I'd have loved to be able to walk down a high street and see him in some plush wine bar like I had before, young secretary in a short skirt, up on her tiptoes kissing him. I'd storm straight in with my girl and my mates, down shots, tear the place up, have the time of our lives, while he stood watching, running his hands through his hair, agitated to fuck and bitter. Bitter that I wasn't standing next to him with some bird from the office boasting about business deals.

I think the only reason my father left me everything in his will was because he hoped that one day, when everything else I had done had come to nothing, I'd somehow find my way into his chair and make him proud. That's the only reason I can think of, because before he died, he despised me.

Things came to a head between us when I was fourteen. I'd been in private school for about three years. Despite additional tutoring, my grades were getting worse and worse. I was still harbouring hopes that he'd send me to the comprehensive my friends had gone to after St George's, even though it would've been difficult to fit in, it would have been better than where I was.

It was a couple of days after some exam results that my father and I had our biggest bust-up. I was standing in the kitchen, fixing a sandwich, when he came in from work. He was red-faced, had no tie on and I immediately knew he'd been to a corporate do all afternoon. My only surprise was that he didn't have a young secretary with him. In the past, when I'd seen him drunk so early in the evening, after being introduced to his female 'business colleague' I'd go straight to my room and keep the headphones on so I couldn't hear them at it.

This time, because he had nothing else to entertain him, he wouldn't let me past.

My father sat at the table and stretched his legs out.

I picked my sandwich up and went to step over his legs but he lifted them up.

I stepped back and waited.

He continued staring at me.

I tried again, and again he lifted his legs, catching me

on the shins.

I leant back against the kitchen bench and started eating my sandwich.

His eyes were heavy and bloodshot, his mouth thin and turned down.

I was curious to hear what terrible life lay ahead of me now that I was officially a loser.

The only sounds were the kitchen clock ticking and the fridge humming.

I kept catching his stares, holding the gaze long enough to let him know I wasn't bothered what he had to say.

His lip curled up at one side into a cruel smile. "You're a mistake, you know that, don't you?"

I kept eating my sandwich – slow, deliberate bites.

He pushed himself up using the table, opened the glass cabinet and made himself a gin and tonic. He sat back down, snipped the end off his cigar and rolled it between his fingers.

I finished eating, turned my back on him and began making some orange juice.

"Your mother trapped me. Fucking bitch. Should have seen it coming."

"More like you trapped her," I muttered.

"You what?'

"Nothing."

"What did you just say?"

I picked my drink up and as I stepped over his legs, he kicked me hard in the stomach. I kicked him back and he sprung out of his seat, grabbing me by the neck and shoulders.

"You're a fucking embarrassment!"

I swung my elbow back to get him off me and cracked him in the face and we both fell back over onto the floor. I was up quick but he grabbed my ankle, his long nails digging into my skin.

I broke away, ran up stairs and locked myself in the bathroom.

He screamed and shouted, and smashed up the kitchen.

I heard a door slam, but I didn't go to the window to see him. I'd spent years at the front window waiting to see who he brought home. Now I didn't care, and now I knew for sure that he didn't care about me either.

* * *

I'd been awake a while, squirming on my back, shielding my eyes from the sun, before I sat forward. I felt well rough. The cavalry soldiers next to us had been replaced by a quartet of hippies jamming with a guitar. The one bunked right up to me had blond scruffy dreadlocks matted together with red beads, and stank of sweat and whatever else hippies dowse themselves in to smell so bad.

A bottle of water appeared in front of me, courtesy of one of them. I thanked him and downed most of the bottle. At least they recognised a daytime hangover when they saw one. What I needed was a beer to take the edge off.

Amber pulled herself up using my knee and said she felt ill.

The hippies obliged with the water again.

I've got to say, apart from the prick that tried to tap Amber up, everyone we'd met at the festival had been spot-on. I've never known such warmness and generosity. They'd welcomed us so much that I now felt like one of them.

Amber and I propped each other up and drifted off, people watching.

Four lads, wearing red shorts and painted silver from head to toe, were playing hand tennis against the monument. From what I could gather by the high-fives being dished out, to win a point the ball had to come back off the stairs and pass the opposing team. If the ball hit the top of a step or whatever on a serve and went skew-whiff, the point was played again. I watched them for ages, totally engrossed in the tight fought match.

When they stopped for a breather and sat up on the steps, I became agitated, not agitated, puzzled. What was I trying to work out here? Why was I still staring at the skinny lad after the game had finished? Why had I been rooting for him to win and not the others?

"I don't believe it."

Amber had been watching something else. "What's up?"

"Check out the lads out playing tennis."

"What about them?"

"You not notice anything strange about them?"

Amber studied them, then clasped a hand over her mouth.

"Jesus no! It can't be!"

"It is. That there in all his glory is our very own Cam Brazelle."

"Eh? Eeee! Yeah! I never noticed him, I saw Gregg first. How fat?"

I was gobsmacked. The rugby player with the bouncing silver tits and love handles was Gregg! I swear I would never have sussed him if I sat there for a month!

When the game resumed we were glued, rolling over laughing as the two of them went at it, and they were going great guns, high –fiving and bumping bellies like true champs. When they huddled together to discuss tactics they looked like David and Goliath, two silver warriors using finesse and brute force to overcome the enemy. They were taking the game so seriously, it was hilarious, and we were right into it too, desperate for them to win.

There was another break in the action so we headed over, thanking the hippies as we left. They were sat on the steps in the shade.

Cam saw us and ran over, flinging his arms around Amber like he hadn't seen her in years.

"Where the hell you been?" he said, grabbing me.

"We've not moved from here. Where you been?"

Gregg came tumbling down the steps with his silver arms outstretched like a steel girder. After crushing us in a sweaty headlock and smothering us in kisses, he stepped back, arms outstretched again. "Fucking class, or what?"

"Class, or what?" Cam repeated, standing alongside him.

The last time I'd seen Gregg he was apprehensively following Cam, swearing blind that if any of the weirdoes came near him he'd do them properly – *no questions asked.*

Amber and I circled them, like we'd discovered a rare breed of animal in the outback. We'd seen some crazy sights here, but none more so than these two.

"What the hell?" Amber said, hands on hips.

This was probably Cam's dream party, being able to be so open, within reason. But Gregg? Fuck's sakes. I wanted to ask him how the change had come about. How had Fat Tuesday loosened him up so much in a few hours? How had being here made him strip to a pair of red shorts and prance around with THAT body, and not give a shit? Amber wrapped her arms around my neck and kissed my cheeks and forehead and then lips, and I realised it wasn't my place to ask that of anyone.

"Give them one, then," Gregg said.

Cam jogged to the stairs and returned with a purple, green and gold haversack. He glanced over his shoulder, then brought out a tiny clear plastic bag.

"Don't be alarmed," he said, all hands. "It's tremendous gear. We've had one each and feel great."

"What is it?" I asked.

"Harry Potters."

"Harry Potters?"

"You never heard of Harry Potters?" Gregg said, taking a pill out of the bag. He reached for the water and necked it. "The best you can get. No side-effects."

Amber took her shades off. "Yeah, *but-what-are-they*? If it's anything like acid, you can count me out."

"And me. It'll be far too tricky here on acid and don't forget we're in hiding, gents."

"It's E," Cam explained. "Totally mellow, everybody's into it, look." He opened the little bag and there were about twenty white tablets branded with a pair of glasses.

"What's it like mixed with beer?" I asked.

Gregg gave us a reassuring hug and whispered, "Even better with beer."

Cam said that the buzz was much more subtle compared to acid. A completely different high that gave you boundless energy and made you want to dance all night. I'd read once that a girl died taking E and that dehydration was a major factor in her body not being able to cope. Cam reckoned that they often laced the E with all sorts of shit, but these ones were pure – or close to.

He also said, with a wink, that E made you horny as fuck. My mind jumbled up at that point and a mixture of Amber and me in the tent was being rudely interrupted by flashes of Cam being *horny as fuck* with the cavalry soldiers and hippies. I shivered and had to stop thinking about being horny all together.

Gregg said it would take an hour to work, by which time they would have finished playing doubles and a parade was due to start.

Amber and I took one pill each and headed for the entrance to go see Teatime, arranging to meet at the monument in forty-five minutes.

* * *

Teatime had been waiting patiently by the tent door for us and he turned himself inside out when he saw us. We fed him, topped his water bowl up and sat with him for a while and laughed about those two playing tennis.

Amber confessed that she thought, but she wasn't sure, and I wasn't to say anything, that Cam *might* be gay. She had her suspicions before, but after seeing him here, she thought, but wasn't sure, that he *might* swing both ways. I promised I wouldn't say anything.

Gregg led the way along Riverside Road, passed St Michael's Square and into the bottom end of Abbotsvale. The streets here seemed even narrower than at the top end and the temperature dropped significantly. The buildings were all terraces and constructed with grey and pink slate. The slate was about two inches thick and laid at such an angle it gave the impression that the buildings were leaning in over, closing out even more light.

The hike was all up hill and we stopped for a rest at the first crossroads.

The next street was darker again and a couple of prostitutes were leaning against a wall, smoking. One of them must have been in her late-fifties and was wearing a big gold belt pulled tight to hide her gut and push the wrinkled flesh up into her bra to pass as a pair of tits. After we passed, they went back inside.

The street was empty, save for a black man on the other side. He was wearing a fur body warmer and white wellies; it had to be the same one we saw on the flyover on the way in. When he saw us, he crossed over and we noticed he wasn't wearing anything down below. I stepped onto the road, pulling Amber with me and focused on the ball of light ahead.

"Aye, aye," Gregg said, as the bloke passed. "Did you see the size of his tool?"

Cam was on the road with us. "Obviously not on the E, is he?"

My face was burning up. I wasn't sure if it was the beer sweating out, the uphill power walking, the E kicking in, or all three. I was on edge, hemmed in and short of breath. This part of town was for the lowlifes, a no-go area for the public. That's why we hadn't seen any police. Each doorway we passed I expected someone to jump out and approach us. It felt like the whole town was rocking apart from this one street.

Reaching the top, we stepped out into the sunlight and civilisation. I glanced back down and after the first few doorways I could only see shadows crossing the street.

We made our way towards the fountain and took refuge outside The Milestone pub. There were stalls set out in a horseshoe around one side of the fountain, and a few more behind in the small grassed park, selling everything from cakes and Indian head massages to Mardi Gras clothing and CDs.

Gregg went over to two girls sat at their stall. They were nude to the waist, painted green and wearing blonde wigs. For $20, they painted people silver, gold or green, or I guess a combination of the three. He bummed a light off one of them and as he did the girl yanked him towards her and they began necking furiously. When she'd finished devouring him, she slapped him on the backside and sent him back over.

"I swear to God," he said. "I'll *never* miss a Fat Tuesday – *ever*."

The painted girls beckoned me over. I shook my head and pointed at Amber, but they were adamant. Amber and I walked over.

"Half price for you two lovers, seeing as it's your first time."

Was it that obvious? I checked myself out in the pub window: adidas trainers, washed-out jeans, Zorro mask pulled down onto my neck and a grubby white t-shirt – hardly outrageous. I sat down and they both went to work on me. When they had finished the top half, the cheekier of the girls started unbuttoning my jeans. I grabbed her hand. Fuck that, I wasn't strolling around in shorts, not with my legs.

Amber was pacing next to me. "Go on! Get "em off!"

The girls joined in the chant, along with Gregg and Cam. I couldn't believe Amber was being so brazen. I let go of the girl's hand and screamed at Cam to go buy me some shorts.

The girls grabbed a leg each and I held on tight to my boxers, conscious of the shrivel I had on. The E could have kicked in, the drink, instant fear of my trousers being taken down by strangers, fuck knows, but it wasn't happening downstairs.

This changed in an instant when the cheekier of the girls started painting the tops of my thighs. She hiked my boxers up and painted using her hands in a gentle massaging motion. When she'd finished, she leant forward to whisper in my left ear. I lowered my head, blocking Amber's view of my right side. The girl slipped her hand inside my boxers, took a hold, and squeezed hard four times. After the last squeeze she gave it three slow pulls and one sharp, before standing up. "Now you have a good one, won't you?" she said, smiling.

Amber was bouncing around, ecstatic at what I looked like, oblivious to the tent in my lap. The quieter of the girls steered me to the seat opposite, where I quickly leant forward, praying it would go down.

Amber was next up, all smiles, laughing with the girls, until they tried to take her vest off. "No, no, just the arms and legs, thanks."

The cheeky girl sat back. "You've got to be out of your mind," she said, then leaning forward and feeling Amber's tits with both hands. "What I would give for these."

Amber was rigid.

I jumped up. "Go on! Who gives a shit?"

Her eyes darted between the girls and me, and she lifted her arms up with a shriek. "I can't believe I'm doing this!"

She looked petrified.

"Put your vest back on, honey," the quieter of the girls said, when they'd finished. "That way you can flash for your beads." She winked at Amber and launched her bra into a cheering crowd of St Trinian girls.

Amber and I thanked them, and walked a few steps towards Cam and Gregg and stopped. I had goosebumps round the back and side of my head and along my jawline. My heart was racing. I could hardly catch my breath. My face was tingling, down my neck and shoulder....

"You're rushing," Cam was saying, arm over my shoulders. "The best or what?"

The goosebumps drained from my face down through

my body.

Amber clung to me as the four of us formed a silver scrum.

"You ok?" I asked her.

"I'm not sure, I'm not sure, it's good, it's good, I'm not sure."

"First one takes it out of you," Cam said. "The next will be the best feeling you ever had, my friend."

"Fucking class or what?" Gregg said, pulling us all closer together.

I don't know how long that first rush lasted, but it sapped everything out of Amber and me. We kept hold of each other, heads bowed together, stroking our own faces and neck, letting the feeling run through us.

Everything went quiet around us.

A voice echoed through a megaphone: "Marasa 69! Freedom! Justice! Peace!"

The roar of the crowd from somewhere behind us was followed by heavy drums and air horns as the parade got underway. Amber and I stood together like a boulder caught in rapids as everyone surged past us.

Gregg and Cam came back for us.

It was ten deep leading up to East Road and we could only see flashes of the parade passing between buildings. I kept tight hold of Amber and we made for the square, then up onto East Road. We were about five from the front, everyone pushing and shoving, trying to get closer, before we saw the procession. A King Kong sized *Lone Ranger* wearing a studded dog collar, with three stone goddesses on clouds, either side. This was by far the biggest and best trailer we'd seen. It must have been over twenty-feet high and half the width of the road.

The people riding the trailer were dressed as super heroes and villains. Batmans and Robins, Superman, The Penguin, and they were going crazy, hanging right over the sides and pulling hysterical people aboard. The only ones acting with any dignity were the King and Queen at the very front, with their handheld masks, elegantly waving to the crowd. The earlier parades had joined the back and The Tractor Boys were drowning out everything else.

Amber's eyes were wild and black, her lips bright red. "We've got to get something!" she yelled. "Come on!"

We were front row now, in line with the Marasa Pride banner, held aloft by two men dressed as Wonder Woman.

I tried everything to get them to throw me something, but I wasn't getting noticed at all. Silver and naked was the norm here.

Amber was having no joy either, but she was determined. After another blank she pushed passed a policeman, dipped under the guide rope and screamed at Batman. The masked crusader looked down at her and she whipped her vest off and offered up her tits. He beckoned her over, and she jumped up and collected something from him.

She pushed her way out, screaming for me. I guided her to safety and she opened her palm to reveal a gold coin with two bare-chested masked men on one side, Marasa Stone 69 around the edge, and Fat Tuesday on the other side. Freedom, Justice, Peace on the rim.

"Spence!" Cam yelled. "Quick!"

We zigzagged towards him.

The main parade had passed and the big screen in the square was now showing The Lone Ranger heading down Riverside Road and Gregg was being hugged and kissed aboard the Marasa 69 trailer. His green wig bobbing through the super heroes like a static balloon.

We chased after them down the bank, under the flyover and onto Riverside Road. Gregg appeared at the back wearing a red and gold fur trimmed crown and matching cloak. He shook his staff at us, before being dragged away.

"What the fuck?" I said, hands on knees.

Amber flopped over my back. "H-how did he manage that?"

We started back up the hill.

"You know what a greedy sod he is," Cam panted. "Well, they were giving these cakes out at the front."

"King Cakes?" Amber said.

"Must be. Anyway, he takes two, scoffs one and bites into the other, spits it into his hand and picks out this little white doll. The woman giving the cakes out grabs hold of him and drags him away."

"Must be a prize for getting it," I said. "I wonder if

he gets anything else?'

"He'll be hoping for more cake," Amber said.

We stopped for a breather just down from the stone arch that led back to the campsite.

"You've got a great pair of tits, Amber," Cam said, leaning against the wall. "No wonder you got that coin."

Amber leant into me, slightly turning her back to Cam. "And they're all yours," she said, pushing me into the doorway.

Kissing frantically, I spun her and slammed her against the shop door. She wrapped her legs around my waist and I forced myself hard up against her. She tore my shorts down past my knees and I yanked hers to one side...

Cam was nudging me in the back. "Spence. Spence! The police are four steps away and counting."

Amber lowered her feet to the floor and we straightened ourselves out and walked up the bank.

Cam was talking but I wasn't listening. All I wanted was to get Amber into the tent.

Before I knew what was happening, the three of us were walking along the straw track and Amber was on her knees cuddling Teatime. Shit! I wanted to be alone with her, spend the rest of the night in the tent.

"Told you it made you horny," Cam said, sitting crossed legged, knocking up.

"You're not kidding."

I guzzled half-a-litre of water and smoked a joint

with Cam while Amber was sorting herself out. I expected her in jeans and t-shirt, baseball cap back on. Opportunity gone.

Our tent door opened and Amber was kneeling up, wearing only black knickers. She slowly raised her index finger and I was summoned.

17

The big wheel over next to the Tarstan River started to turn and a huge cheer went up. Amber and I got some clothes on and came out.

Amber lit us both a smoke and we downed a bottle of water between us.

I'd bitten away all the inside of one cheek and began chewing on the other.

The campsite had a thick layer of grey smoke, just above head height, blowing over it and it stank of burning hay or some other farm shit. Just about every tent had a ghetto blaster on full tilt and a couple of steps either way and you'd be listening to a different tune.

Cam was talking to a Goth, who had a sign outside her tent saying 'The Devil Loves'; the *L* of love was painted red with blood drops pooling beneath it.

Amber and I grabbed a towel each and made our way to the toilet block to get cleaned up. There were no showers, but we managed to scrub most of the silver off.

I had no real buzz now, just loads of energy.

When we came back, Cam was sat stroking Teatime, knocking up. Amber bent down and kissed him. "Still having a good time?"

He glanced up long enough to cop another smacker of Amber.

Amber went back inside to get ready and I sat next to Cam.

He gave me the joint and started making another.

I'll tell you one thing about being on E: you're constantly active. There's no down time or chilling out. For me it was smoking, drinking water and pacing around in a small area never too far from the tent. For Cam, knocking joints up and talking to groups of people. Any groups. He'd just head over to total strangers and start cracking on, nothing was a problem. His little outings usually ended with hugs and kisses, and he was back, singing the praises of the people he'd met and telling us their business.

Amber was all lovey. Apart from being stuck to me and constantly glossing her lips, she felt the need to kiss Cam, which of course I had no problem with, every time she clapped eyes on him. On his return from the toilet, he was cuddled and kissed and given water and guided to a comfortable patch of grass to sit on. Her mothering instincts were on overdrive and all our clothes were neatly folded in the tent. Teatime was full and content at our feet.

It had been a couple of hours since we'd seen Gregg and we were taking it in shifts to stand on the straw track and keep a look out. As time got on, we started to seriously worry that something was amiss. That was until Cam shouted us up onto the track.

"Check this out," he said, pointing.

I squinted at the figure blazing a trail towards us, forcing people off the side of the track. "Is that a lass with him?"

"It's a little'n if it is."

Gregg's fur crown was cocked to one side, his cloak wafting up behind him as he strode towards us. His gut wobbled with every step and the girl he was dragging along was doing four steps to his one by the look of it. Any faster and she'd be on her back, heels scraping the ground as The King dragged home the day's catch.

On reaching us, he gave us a twirl. "They insisted on painting The King gold, it's tradition." He babbled on about the ceremony, sweating like fuck, arms all over, still holding onto the girl. "Eh, this is Dewy."

"Julie, cheeky." The little Asian girl broke free and shook our hands. "Shall we?" she said to Gregg.

"Oh, yes."

We followed them back to the tents.

Without another word, Gregg drove his staff into the ground, hung his cloak and crown on it, unzipped his tent and showed the girl in.

I swear it was like a cartoon scrap in there, arms and legs bulging the tent, 'Ooooing' and 'Aaaaring' like they were treading hot coals. "Ah yes... aaaah that's it... fucking hell... aah yes, fucking hell... aaaaah... fucking hell... go on..."

"Have you h-heard him?" Cam managed, holding onto me.

"Aaaaah… fucking hell… Jesus… aaaah…"

The fracas only lasted a couple of minutes.

We were just recovering when the girl's head popped out and honest to God it wasn't the same person: massive hair, scarlet face and tiny red tits. "You haven't got a ciggie, have you?"

That did me right in and I rolled into a ball laughing so hard I nearly spewed. I straightened up for a second and saw the Pekinese face and cave woman hair and was over again, begging for mercy.

The gold beachball emerged over the top and finished us off. "Make a joint, man, it's hard graft being The King."

By the time we had recovered, Gregg and Julie were sitting in front of us smoking. Life would have been so much easier if either of them had changed their appearance, but The King was sat there like a gold Buddha and Julie was merrily chuffing away with her little red tits on show. Every time Cam looked up he lost it big time.

Julie pointed at me for about the tenth time. "So you're, Spence, and you're…"

"Caaaaaam – I'm sorry."

"And…"

"Amber."

Gregg went back inside and Cam wandered off,

claiming he needed the toilet.

Julie was a great laugh and had us enthralled with tales of festivals she had been to and her methods of pulling men. Without any shame, she told us that Gregg was number three this weekend and was definitely the best, but a bit rough.

"I put that down to the doves though," she said, disappearing behind a mushroom of smoke. "They make *me* randy as hell, so lads must be bursting on them."

"Doves?" Cam said, sitting back down.

"Yeah, you not had any doves? See Arthur, he swapped me two for two Harry Potters. It'll not do me any harm to keep off them for a while, I'll miss all the bands at this rate."

"Oh, Arthur!" Cam shouted.

"Anyway, I best get back, the girls will be worried. We're over there in line with the house if you want to call over later."

There was another quick scuffle in the tent before she left.

"Oh, Arthur."

Gregg lumbered out and stretched, his nasty blue underpants riding up his arse, showing the great white-gold divide.

"I'll tell you what," he said, "she was a right little raver."

Gregg had been doing some wheeling and dealing, and had decided we were heavy on uppers and light on downers, so he swapped some E for a quarter of skunk and some Temazepan. He was standing proud in his cloak and crown, hands on hips, checking the rest of the campsite out.

"Every time I talk to someone they offer me something for nothing, Spence. And there are guaranteed privileges being King."

"Like what?"

"I can't remember everything but I definitely get on the rides for nothing, it's unreal – no sooner do I stand still and I'm surrounded, have one of these, take one of those, bottles of water. That's how I pulled little Dewy. She dropped a dove in my mouth when I lifted her up for a kiss."

"You've had doves already?" Cam said. "How many? And where are ours?"

"Simmer. I've had one."

"How many?"

"One dove and two bombs. I swear that's it," hands up, "and I've got plenty for us, two ticks."

Gregg pulled a small plastic bag from his cloak and handed us each a white tablet.

"Dancey as fuck these. I must have lost two stone marching around and doing my duty as King between the sheets. Did I tell you about Dewy on the waltzer? She's a right little raver."

"I'm not taking any more," Amber said. "This is our first time and we've already had one and loads of smoke."

Cam washed his down. "You'll be fine. Just don't have any more after this."

"What's the chances of OD'ing on these?" I asked.

"They can catch up with you, but a couple's fine, Spence, just don't have any more."

Amber and I weren't sure what to do, so I took the two tablets and put them in my pocket for later.

Gregg mumbled something and staggered towards me.

"Here... I've got you," I said, lowering him to the ground.

Cam removed his cloak and crown, and he lay with his head in Amber's lap and she stroked his hair. His eyes flickered, then rolled back, leaving the bloodshot whites. I gently poured some water in his mouth but it spilled back out.

Cam beckoned me over to Gregg's tent.

"Have you seen this?" he said, opening the cloak.

It was like a medicine cabinet: brown bottles, a blue bottle, skunk, white and brown tablets, brown capsules and white powder.

After sniffing and tasting the contents of one of the opaque bottles, Cam held it between his thumb and index finger and said, "This is GHB, I'm sure of it."

"What's GHB?"

"Liquid E. And this little one's poppers. I'm confiscating the lot. He'll OD, Spence. Liquid E hits you in minutes, so he's probably been topping himself up with rushes all afternoon. Here, you take the poppers and GHB and I'll take the rest."

I stuffed them into my pockets and turned around. Amber was still nursing Gregg.

I had a drink of water, sparked a smoke up, and walked up onto the straw track with Teatime.

The sun was a fireball spreading across the skyline; above it, the sky was clear blue, above that, the sparse clouds were tinged with red, giving the effect of a blue mountain with red peaks. I lifted my face up, expecting to feel its warmth, but the temperature was dropping.

The campsite was starting to empty.

I could hear faint screams coming from the big wheel.

I watched two girls, goths or hippies with long pleated black dresses and long black hair, argue over a multi-coloured scarf.

I went back to the tents.

Gregg was jaw wobbling, one story mixing into another. Eventually he lost it all together and got upset. "I love you all, you know. I'd be lost without you."

Amber cuddled and kissed him, then Cam and finally me.

The roller coaster he was riding suddenly hit a high and he jumped up and grabbed his cloak. "What the fuck we doing sitting here? Are we going to party or what? Shit! Hold on." He dashed in and out of his tent. "There are loads of police down on the main street so I got you these." He held up three masks.

"What are they?" I asked, taking one.

"Michael Hutchence face masks."

"I thought he died?"

"Tribute band. He's massive over here. Got them for $2 each."

We all declined his offer, pulled our Zorro masks on and made for the stone arch.

Gregg was adamant he was going over to the big wheel. He'd been there earlier and there were rides, a dance tent, the bands and the bungee jump, *and*, as King, he'd probably get on for nothing. We kissed him off, agreeing to meet at Alexanders in the town square in an hour.

The atmosphere in the square was much more chilled than earlier. Without the craziness of the parades, people were happy to be in one place, getting pissed and having a good time. We queued outside the tall, tinted glassed front of Alexanders. There were four bouncers in black suits and red bowties on the door. From what I could see, it didn't look too busy inside, with most people getting served and coming back out.

We edged past the bouncers and Cam went straight over to some lads he'd met earlier, and I made for the bar and ordered us a Jager Bomb each. It was dark inside, low ceilings, lots of standing room, and, at the back, some tan leather armchairs next to an unlit open fire.

While I was waiting, I watched a couple at the end of

the bar get a bottle of champagne in a silver ice bucket. They excitedly chinked champagne flutes and downed the first glass in one. I dipped into my pockets to see if I had enough cash to copy. No cash. Not a penny – I'd given it all to Kyle at the Trinity. I dashed back to Amber, got some money and ordered the champers.

When I returned, Cam was in a deep conversation with a dark haired lad next to the fruit machine and Amber was watching, expecting some activity any second. We dusted off the champagne and got another bottle, with an extra glass for Cam's mate.

An hour later, Amber and I were pissed and all over each other, close to consummating our relationship for the second time in the day. Cam broke us up and I staggered through the now heaving crowd towards the bar.

Standing there, I turned and looked through the bobbing heads trying to see Amber. 50 Cent's *In Da Club* was blasting out of a speaker right next to my head. I ordered the champagne and kept looking.

The young barmaid tapped my arm and mumbled something about going downstairs. I nodded and stood up on the bar footrest, trying to find Amber. I was about to ditch the drinks order and head over when I saw her come out of the toilets. I waved but she couldn't see. I stepped down and waited for the champagne.

I felt uneasy and got back up on the footrest. I scanned the room and immediately spotted the prick with the spiky black hair and red basketball vest. He was head and shoulders above everyone and stood right in front of Amber, arm protectively stretched out like before. Fucker had some nerve. I kept watching, glancing over my shoulder for the barmaid.

The fucker bent down towards her and I was off into the crowd... bouncing off pillars and chairs, drinks flying... suddenly I flew back over, heels trailing along the floor as the bouncer dragged me backwards in a headlock. He was choking me, tightening his grip every time I struggled. He was crushing my windpipe and I couldn't breathe.

He threw me out onto the street and I landed face down, gasping for air. I knelt up, palms on the pavement, coughing and gulping. The queue at the door were cheering. I got to my feet, staggered towards them and demanded to be back in. *I need to be back in! My girlfriend's in trouble! At least tell her I'm out here, you wankers!* All four bouncers stepped forward, staring me out, desperate for an excuse to cave my head in.

I ran up the street, hung a left along an alley, then left again and back down to the rear of Alexanders. I darted round the side to where Amber was standing and banged on the window, screaming her name. The lads were crowding her and I couldn't see her face. I kept screaming and banging, but no one looked. The lad with the tattoo reached for his drink and I caught a glimpse of Amber anxiously looking for me, clutching the champagne glass tight to her chest with both hands.

Cam was pointing at the bar, trying to explain

something to one of the lads. The fucker with the tattoo stepped in from the side and punched Cam in the face and he went flying into some empty chairs and slid to the floor. Amber went into a frenzy, kicking and punching everything in front of her. The lad forced a hand over her mouth and lifted her off the floor and walked her further into the corner while the others watched his back.

I'd been frantically searching for something to smash the window with and was about to take on the bouncers at the front, when the fire exit to my right swung open. I tore through it, knocking the chef aside and sprinted towards them. Rounding the corner next to the fruit machine I snatched a pint glass off the table and rushed the fucker, driving the empty glass straight up into his neck and twisting it hard as my momentum sent us both crashing to the floor. As we hit the deck I bit into his face and head and dug my thumbs into his throat...

I stopped punching when my arm got caught on a barstool. I grabbed the stool by the metal legs and jumped up and smashed it over his head with everything I had, again and again and again...

Cam and Amber were dragging me away, through the fire exit door, down the street, along an alley, then another. I was looking for him at every turn to see if he wanted some more. Amber was in my arms, crying, telling me how much she loved me. Cam was peering around the corner.

My ears popped.

We were stood next to some green industrial bins. It was dark. An image of the fucker carrying Amber into the corner flashed into my mind and I wanted to go back to Alexanders.

I asked Amber if she was okay. She said she was, thanks to me. And that she loved me more than anything. And she begged me not to go back.

Cam was pacing up and down the alley. "Spence, we've got to get out of here! What the hell were you thinking of? You could have killed that lad! You might have! What the fuck were you thinking of!"

I pinned Cam to the wall by his throat. He was choking, kicking at my shins. When he stopped struggling I let him go and he fell to his knees, coughing and spluttering.

Amber helped him up.

I walked to the end of the alley. In front of me was the park, lit-up by street lamps along the footpaths. It was empty save for a couple sat on the steps at the monument, drinking. A group of people were jogging up the bank towards us. Music was thumping from a bar further up on the corner. Fireworks exploded and crackled in the sky behind the big wheel.

Cam tapped me on the shoulder. He handed me his t-shirt. "You can't walk around covered in blood, Spence."

Amber wiped as much blood off me as she could and I put Cam's blue t-shirt on.

We were in the middle of Monument Boulevard.

We cut through the park and made our way up East Road Boulevard towards the stone arch. Cam was in front with Amber. They went through the arch and I kept on walking until I could see the square. There were three ambulances outside Alexanders, police all over it. I turned around and walked back down the bank.

Teatime ran along the track towards me and I knelt down and gave him a hug. I kept checking over my shoulder; they'd come looking for sure. I would. When I reached the tent, Amber was packing our stuff and Cam was pacing, staring at the ground.

I sat down.

Cam stood next to me, huffing and puffing. "What the hell's wrong with you, Spence? Christ's sakes, you glassed three people!"

I didn't answer, just kept my eye on the stone arch waiting for them to come. Cam was shitting himself, banging on and on about me glassing three people. I didn't, I glassed one, who, at the time, was trying to rape my girlfriend.

"Make a joint." I said to Cam.

He kept on rambling and was near hysterical by the time Amber shot out of our tent.

"MAKE A FUCKING JOINT! MAKE A JOINT! HE'S PROTECTING ME! CAN'T YOU SEE THAT! PROTECTING ME! NOW MAKE A FUCKING JOINT!"

Cam sat down and began knocking up.

I went up onto the track.

There were a group of lads congregating at the entrance. One of them broke away and ran along the track shouting something over and over. I went back to the tents.

"Where's that camping knife," I asked Cam. He wouldn't look up, just kept rolling the joint.

Amber went down on her hands and knees and rummaged through the camping gear. "Here," she said, handing me the knife. It was an eight-inch Bowie knife, which Gregg had insisted we buy to cut food, hunt animals and fend of homs. I got a feel for it, then tucked it into my jeans and walked up onto the track.

Cam followed, offering me the joint. He spoke softly. "Spence, look. Think what you're doing. Let's just calm down, get our stuff and get out of here."

"That's one of them, isn't it?"

It was one of them. He was marching on adrenaline looking for the lad that had done his mate. Well, he'd found him.

Cam was still talking when I pushed him aside.

The lad saw me and I walked towards him, steady pace. Amber appeared alongside me carrying the lump hammer for knocking the pegs in. The lad looked behind him, then back at me. Amber went on the outside and I kept walking straight for him.

Twenty feet away, he checked over his shoulder again, then turned on his heels and legged it.

I kept watching until he was out of sight.

We went back and collapsed the tents.

Gregg came running into camp, still in cloak and crown. "What's happening? Where are the tents? Alexanders is closed. I thought –"

I placed a hand on his shoulder. "Your stuff's over there. We're leaving. Now."

"Leaving? You're having a laugh, the bands have only just started and the number of birds I've…" he looked around, confused. "What's happened?"

We headed for the car in silence, Amber and Teatime flanking me, the other two ahead. Gregg was like a big kid, looking for sympathy because he was tripping on magic mushrooms. We made it to the car. Amber and I jumped in the back with Teatime. Cam was driving with Gregg up front.

As Cam fumbled the keys into the lock, we were blinded by torches, people screaming at us to put our hands on our heads. The car doors swung open and we were dragged out by the police, pinned to the floor and arrested on suspicion of robbing Vasey supermarket.

Part Three

18

On arrival at Marasa Police Headquarters, the police surgeon examined me, and photographed and recorded my injuries (cuts to my back, hands and arms, swollen face, bust lip), before passing me fit for interview. If I required any medication, only the police surgeon could administer it. Once booked in, I was strip-searched, swabbed and fingerprinted and all my clothes taken for forensics. I was locked up in a video camera cell wearing a blue paper suit. I sat on the bed, back to the officer keeping me company.

Nothing else happened for a while apart from me demanding water and reciting the dangers of being dehydrated on drugs, and ranting about the police surgeon's incompetence at passing me fit for interview. They'd found drugs on me, so I was using this to try and buy some time so my head could clear and I could concentrate solely on the robbery. The surgeon was of the opinion that I had been intoxicated earlier in the evening, but was now fit for interview.

The police from Sydney were already there ready to

interview me. I had delayed proceedings by requesting my own solicitor instead of the stiff they had lined up. Peter Simms got in touch with another one of my father's business colleagues, who was semi-retired and living in Brisbane. Gavin Hopper was in his late-fifties, early-sixties, over six feet, slim and balding with grey tufty wings. His face and head were narrow and long, like a beaker. I've met him a couple of times at our house and he'd stayed once for Christmas dinner, so it was no surprise to see the look of disgust on his face when I was escorted into the interview room in handcuffs, looking rough.

After a brief onslaught of what he thought of the situation, and what this would have done to my father, he got down to business. In the disclosure, they hadn't given much away, but mentioned that there was a good chance of someone turning Queen's Evidence against me. Hopper doubted they had any forensics. I asked him about the drugs they had found on me (two E, GHB and poppers).

"You're young and impressionable, Spencer. The drugs are for personal use, and packaged accordingly. There's nothing there that suggests intent to supply. You'll be charged with possession and fined. As for the knife, it was for camping and was only on your person in transit to the car. A grey area at best. They'll get nowhere fast with that, either."

The robbery: I was a very wealthy young man – no motivation for the crime. Worse scenario, if they had forensics, I was in with the wrong crowd and misled. I asked him about Amber and the others, but he could only speculate that they probably didn't have their own counsel and had been interviewed already.

"They can insinuate what the hell they like, Spencer," he said, walking behind my chair. "They can call you a liar over and over, but remember they *cannot – tell – lies.*"

"What if –"

"Facts! They can't say one of your friends has fingered you if they haven't. Do not get involved. Look at me before you reply to every question. If it doesn't involve the robbery, then don't answer."

"Do you think I'll walk out of here tonight?"

"Until we know what they've got, I couldn't say."

He kept circling me, hands together behind his back. "They'll use bullyboy tactics, Spencer. I expect them to go right at you, but they have to be careful, if they cross the line and become oppressive, the interview will become non-admissible." He leant over the table. "Do not get involved! Don't let them get your goat. I'm here to protect you, so don't try to prove your innocence. It's only the result that matters, not what they think."

The custody officer led me back to my cell.

I was worried about Amber. The adrenaline had been pumping when we were arrested and I'd had extra time to calm down. She would have been taken straight into the interview room I expect, half looking over her shoulder for the fuckers that tried to rape her. No matter what image came into my mind – the robbery, what evidence they had, my stupidity for doing it, getting out of here, Amber and I together, how cool she was, how much I loved her, being together for the rest of our lives, the tent – it was soon replaced with Amber being lifted into the corner in Alexanders. A constant throbbing reminder that made my guts turn of how close I came to failing the one person I care about.

I was taken back through the holding area, past the line of whinging suspects sat on the wooden benches, along a corridor of steel doors, down a narrow corridor and into an interview room. The room was about ten feet square, tatty brown carpet on the floor and walls, a round table with four chairs fixed to the floor and in the corner, a small wooden box. Hopper stood up and I sat next to him.

Two plain clothed detectives followed me in and sat facing us. One looked quite young, late-twenties, plump, with ginger curly hair. His chubby face was pebble-dashed with freckles. On closer inspection, the pebbledash had a sprinkling of black moles, one of which, on his chin, had sprouted a hair over an inch long. How could he not see that? The other detective was a throwback, hard-drinking, no-nonsense, seen-it-all copper with a purple veiny face. He had dark, greased back hair, thinning at the side, like Dracula. And he stank of BO.

Irwin: "Interview commencing 7.05pm Sunday 6th

September. Present, myself Detective Constable Irwin."

"Detective Sergeant McQueen."

"Gavin Hopper, Brummell, Reid and Hopper."

Irwin: "State your name, date of birth and address."

I gave them my address in Newcastle.

DS McQueen leant forward.

Irwin stared at me. "Did you rob Vasey supermarket on Friday night, 4th September?"

I looked at Hopper and he nodded. "No."

"Interview suspended 7.08." They stood up, stopped the tapes and left the room.

I went to speak but Hopper shook his head.

Fifteen minutes later they returned, started the tapes and resumed the interview.

"Spencer," Irwin said. "You know we're investigating the robbery at Vasey Supermarket on Friday. If you say you're not involved, then tell me in your own words what you did from 1pm that day. Take your time."

I told them about my day at the garage, getting ready for work, clocking in at ten, everything down to having a couple of cans when we got in. It took about ten minutes and DS McQueen scribbled every word down.

"Ok, Spencer," Irwin said. "We'll have a quick break. Interview suspended 7.32."

Ten minutes later they were back.

Irwin: "Ok, Spencer. I just need to go into more detail

so I've got it clear in my mind." I nodded. "Which route did you take to work?"

"We go the same way every night, through the park, Darlinghurst Road, Bourke Street and in the front entrance."

"Why didn't you clock out on Friday night?" McQueen asked.

"We always get a flier on a Friday and take turns clocking the cards. The lad we left the cards with forgot to clock us out."

"Interview suspended 7.46."

They returned fifteen minutes later.

Irwin: "Have you ever been in the secure area in Vasey supermarket, Spencer?"

"Yes."

"When?"

"When I was interviewed."

"How long ago was that?"

"About four, five months, I'm not sure."

"Have you been in since then?"

"No."

"Liar," McQueen said.

"Interview suspended 8.07."

Irwin: "Just tying up some loose ends here, Spencer. Now, which door did you leave through on Friday night?'

"Em, we took the service yard entrance, because we

were going early, it's the only way we wouldn't be seen."

"What time?"

"I'm not sure, about one."

"Interview sus-"

"Oh, for crying out loud!" Hopper shoved his pad away and stood up. "This is preposterous! This strategy will you get you nowhere! He's willing to answer every question relevant to your enquiry, at least show him some bloody respect. Your time is disappearing fast, detective, so if you have anything, then I suggest you bring it to the table or release my client."

"Interview suspended 8.22."

"Interview resumed 8.38."

Irwin: "Ok, Spencer. We're getting there. Were Brazelle and Dawson with you when you left work on Friday night?"

"Yes."

"Who was meant to clock you out?"

"Gregg sorted it, I mean Dawson. He arranged it."

"What time did you get back to 265 Darlinghurst Road after your shift?"

"Not sure, it takes about ten minutes, so about half twelve, quarter-to-one."

McQueen: "There are two doors in the service yard. Which one did you leave by?"

"One next to frozen foods, the other is locked by Jeff."

"Who's Jeff?"

"Maintenance bloke."

"You know him well?"

"No."

"How well?"

"Never spoken to him."

"Been in his office?"

"No."

"No?"

"Interview suspended 8.44."

"Clock's ticking, Sergeant," Hopper said, folding his arms.

McQueen: "We're waiting on forensics to challenge the interview and the Superintendent has already confirmed an extension if we need it. So I wouldn't worry yourself too much about the time."

"Sergeant, my client isn't feeling too good and may need painkillers. If he has painkillers it is likely that he will be unfit for interview. That's the opinion of the police surgeon, you understand.

"Like I said, the clock is ticking and if you don't get on with it my client will be on his way back to his cell. And I want these tactics detailed on his custody record, this is an absolute disgrace.'

Irwin: "Spencer, there're a few discrepancies in your account of Friday night I need to go through. Firstly, you couldn't have left through the door you said, because your immediate supervisor has confirmed that both were locked for the duration of the night."

"As far as I can remember we left that way, we always do when we're –"

"Robbing the place," McQueen said. "You and Dawson are well known for thieving from the store."

"Don't know what you're on about."

"Sergeant, we're here to interview my client, not chat about his acquaintance."

Irwin: "Ok, Spencer, let's say you were mixed up. Why did you leave town on the 1.15 bus. A bit late at night to move on after a shift at work, don't you think?"

"We'd already decided to go and the festival tickets were cheap."

McQueen: "You're a liar, Hargreaves. You're making this all up. You're tripping yourself up at every corner and your so-called mates' versions are completely different. You robbed Vasey supermarket and skipped town."

"Prove it."

They went through everything again from the beginning: stop start, stop start, stop start. I wasn't even sure if I was giving the same answers. Every answer triggered an outbreak of questions. What colour door? Ten minutes or fifteen? How many bags to the station? Who carried them? What colour? How heavy?

Hopper kept on at them and was threatened with an application for a warrant of further retention, which could take up to thirty-six hours.

"Sergeant, regardless of what threats you care to pollute the air with, your line of enquiry must be carried out within the parameters of the law. The detention clock is ticking and my client will be spending the next 4 hours in his cell due to poor health unless you move this on."

There was a knock at the door. A woman police constable entered and handed a piece of paper to McQueen. He read it and passed it to Irwin. "Interviewed terminated. Take him back to his cell."

Morning came and I was escorted back through the holding area to the front desk. The large black clock on the wall read 9:15.

The two plain clothed detectives that had interviewed me came in through the double doors and stood at the exit. There were two uniformed officers either side of me, and the desk sergeant behind the counter. Hopper had said last night that it was likely I'd be charged with possession of class A drugs for personal use and released on bail in the morning.

Something was wrong, though. It was too quiet.

The desk sergeant went through the charges – possession of class A drugs, possession of a bladed article, and I signed a statement. He emptied my belongings onto the counter and I signed for them.

I hesitantly looked around. "Is that it? Am I free to go?"

McQueen walked up to me: "Spencer Hargreaves,

I'm arresting you on suspicion of the murder of Charles Surman-Wells. You are not obliged to say or do anything. Anything you do say or do may be recorded and used in a court of law. Do you understand the charge?"

"Eh?'

"Do you understand the charge?"

"Murder? What you on about? Who the fuck's Surman-Wells?"

"Take him down."

I dug my heels in and struggled to break free as they led me away. "What the fuck's going on! I want my solicitor! GET THE FUCK OFF ME! GET OFF ME!"

19

Charles Surman-Wells was a civil servant from Sydney. Charles Surman-Well's job, before he was beaten and strangled to death, was to investigate benefit fraud. He had been investigating Gregg for dodging rates. My fingerprints had been matched to a set found at the crime scene in Palmer Street. I didn't even try to explain the reason my fingerprints were there until Gavin Hopper arrived.

Hopper was standing in the corner of the interview room facing the wall, hands together behind his back. I sat down at the table. As soon as the officer shut the door he spun around, eyes black and raging, and shot towards me, yelling and banging his fist on the table... *Damn fool! You could go down for life! Guilty or not!* I found him quite amusing and he sensed this and stormed for the door.

"The hell with you! I owe you nothing! You hear me! Nothing!"

"Gavin wait, please," I said, getting up. "I'm only smirking because I know how the prints got there."

He stopped at the door, back to me, weighing up his options.

Chin up, hands behind his back, he slowly walked the perimeter of the room. On reaching me, he sat down, crossing his legs. He stared at me, right hand over his mouth. Once I was suitably uncomfortable, he said, "Before we go any further, I deem it necessary to justify my actions to you.

"I will continue defending you for one reason only: the memory of your father. If at any time you no longer require my services, please say so. Once this is over, I will no longer carry out work for you or Hargreaves Financial. Now," he got up and walked behind me. "Last night we were in the driving seat. The possession of the drugs and knife were minor offences and it's safe to assume that they have no forensic evidence connecting you to the robbery of the supermarket. But what they do have now is forensic evidence linking you to a murder scene. This significantly alters our predicament and we now find ourselves, cap in hand, hoping an explanation from you will not only satisfactorily explain why you were at a murder scene, but that you never played *any* part in the crimes committed."

"It will."

"The police are now in a position of power and it may be that they charge and remand you to keep you off the streets and bring forward the evidence at a later date."

"Even if I'm innocent?"

He sat down in the chair opposite. "Ok. This is the story so far. On Friday night you and your friends leave work early and don't clock out. You then catch the last bus out of town heading north. No goodbyes, no notice given to your landlord, nothing. Hours later the alarm is raised at the supermarket when they find the weekend's takings gone. No sign of forced entry, security videotapes gone, an inside job for certain.

"A day later you get arrested carrying a hunting knife and a pocket full of designer drugs, and are covered in cuts and bruises. Finally, your fingerprints are found at the scene of a murder in the town you've just left." He smacked the table as he got up. "Come on! Do you really think the police are that gullible? They see you as a vigilante for Christ's sakes, with the financial clout to run an army... and now... and now, they have something on you."

"Yeah, but I didn't do anything."

"They don't give a damn! Listen to what I'm telling you, boy! They have forensics. It's likely they'll charge you with something and bring further evidence later."

Hopper settled in the chair with his note pad on his knee. "Tell me everything you know about Charles Surman-Wells."

20

The same two detectives were interviewing me. They were much more relaxed with me than before, and didn't keep stopping and starting the interview. I told them about Charles Surman-Wells coming to the flat, photographing me at the supermarket, Cam following Surman-Wells from the gay club and me getting paranoid and bricking his window. They went back through everything I said in more detail and I got the feeling that my reason for following Surman-Wells in the first place didn't sit well with them.

I asked Hopper on the breaks if Amber had contacted him or if she'd been hanging around in reception for me, but she hadn't. I think if I could have seen her, or even knew she was okay, it would have given me more strength to carry on. As it was, I was on my last legs when they moved onto their second piece of evidence. It was a grey cast of a shoe print, which matched the trainers I'd been wearing when arrested. We burnt everything we wore the night of the robbery, but there was no need to discard anything after bricking a window, it was hardly the crime of the century.

Anyway, the shoe print proved that I had been up

close to the house, next to the side window to be exact, and contradicted my original story of only going into next door's garden to throw the brick. I admitted to listening at the window to make sure I had the right room.

DS McQueen was very passive and didn't respond to anything I said, and simply waited for his colleague to finish taking notes, before methodically moving on. Even when he caught me out with the shoe print, he appeared to accept without suspicion that it was a genuine oversight on my behalf.

After a short break, they started the tape and McQueen said: "At any time did you go into 154 Palmer Street?"

"No. Never."

"You sure?"

"Sure."

"We have DNA taken from blood found in Charles Surman-Wells' room at 154 Palmer Street. Your DNA is a match. Can you explain how your blood came to be in Charles Surman-Wells' room?"

My heart was hammering.

"Take your time," McQueen said.

Hopper's heavy breathing was rattling around the room, one croaky deep sigh after another.

"The only way it could have got in his room," I said, eyeing Hopper. "Is… if… if I bled on the brick. Wait a second!" I yanked one sleeve of the blue paper suit up and showed them the inside of my arm. "I get really bad eczema, have done for years and it often bleeds. That night it was bleeding bad. I remember... ask Amber, my, eh, girlfriend, she noticed it..." I knew how desperate and far-fetched I sounded. "I swear I've never been in 154 Palmer Street or met Charles Surman-Wells. Never.'

They suspended the interview.

They came back in and started the tape.

DS McQueen. "Spencer Hargreaves, I'm charging you with the murder of Charles Surman-Wells. You do not have to say or do anything. Anything you do say or do may be recorded and used as evidence in a court of law. Do you understand that?"

"Please, please, you've got to believe me. I swear I didn't do it. Gavin..." Hopper couldn't look at me. "GAVIN! I DIDN'T DO IT! I DIDN'T DO IT! GAVIN! YOU GOT TO BELIEVE ME! GAVIN! GAVIN!'

Part Four
21

On remand I was locked in my cell twenty-three hours a day. One hour out for exercise, and even that was at the discretion of the prison officers. Every day four cells were opened at the same time and allowed down for breakfast, which was dished up on your tray and taken back and eaten in your cell. Before each meal you were given a tea pack, consisting of two teabags, two sugars, two whiteners and two coffees. If you wanted any privileges, like using the gym or library, you had to fill in an application form in advance. I spent the hour I had out my cell on the phone to Amber.

Each week your account was credited with $20 to live off, and you were allowed a maximum of $120 paid into your account. Amber made sure mine was always full. The real currency in prison was phone cards and tobacco.

I got a letter from Hopper, saying he could no longer represent me, claiming that criminal law was not his speciality. He recommended a barrister from Sydney, who commanded a premium, but was the best. Hopper wished me well and enclosed a self-addressed envelope for my instructions. I wrote back asking him to send my case to the barrister.

Three weeks later I was sat opposite Keith Gallagher going through the case. Keith Gallagher looked young for a barrister, I thought, maybe late-thirties. He was stocky and had poker-straight sandy hair with cow's licks either side, and the biggest and cleanest set of teeth I'd ever seen. I caught him yawning once and his mouth was so big you could drop a cooking apple in it without it touching the sides. He wore a black pin-stripped suit, sharp white shirt with gold cufflinks and yellow tie. The only thing that didn't fit his image was his deep monotone voice – nothing snappy about that at all.

The prosecution had a set amount of time to bring forward the further evidence they claimed to be getting together. Gallagher reckoned a couple of months more and the judge would want to see all the evidence and decide whether there was a case for court – which, Gallagher said, there would be, unless the real killer was brought to justice before then. This was also a possibility as another blood sample had been found on Surman-Wells and some unidentified fingerprints. I was desperate for some good news from Gallagher, even it was just his opinion, but he never mentioned the possibility of me getting out, so I asked him outright and he said, in that drone of a voice, that I shouldn't be thinking about getting out, only about keeping my nose clean and doing my time. The fucker made me feel worse than ever and I got thinking about Amber on the outside without me. What if she found someone else? If she did, I wouldn't be bothered about getting out of here. What would be the point?

Nothing happened for five months, save for I got out of my cell for three to four hours a day, twice-a-week, for recreation. It meant an extra long phone call to Amber and, out of sheer boredom, I started working out in the gym.

I had lots of different cellmates and didn't like any of them. I dare say they didn't like me. Being in a twelve-by-six room with a stranger, usually a total scumbag, for over twenty-hours a day is all about compromise. Three hours of crosswords is better than listening to the grunts and strains of someone taking a shit for an hour. One thing I could never get used to was the junkies. When they first came in, they screamed all night and kept the whole wing awake. I ended up sleeping during the day.

I'd been in the Metropolitan Remand Centre in Sydney for six months when the prosecution submitted the further evidence. Keith Gallagher was now in a position to direct me.

"Spencer, the crown has to prove beyond any reasonable doubt that you took Surman-Wells' life and they have the evidence to do that. What isn't so certain, is *why* you took his life and this is what we must work on in your defence."

"Whoa, whoa," I said, leaning forward. "I didn't kill Surman-Wells. Read what I've said. I've never met the bloke or went into his digs."

"The further evidence they have brought forward is," he pulled a sheet of paper from his briefcase and laid it in front of me, "detailed here. Ignore the fancy jargon and read here. They found skin and blood on Surman-Wells' clothing. That skin and blood is yours. I can't see how you can deny being in a struggle with him and, consequently, whether you meant it or not, killing him."

"I DIDN'T FUCKING DO IT! YOU HEAR WHAT I'M FUCKING SAYING PRICK! I DIDN'T DO IT! I DIDN'T FUCKING DO IT! YOU UNDERSTAND WHAT I'M FUCKING SAYING –"

The screws burst in and dragged me back to my cell.

22

Even though they are not accepted in Australia as proof, I demanded to take a polygraph test and after I refused to change my plea, Gallagher agreed.

I took the test three times and passed three times.

Gallagher now believed that I genuinely thought I hadn't been in 154 Palmer Street and hadn't murdered Charles Surman-Wells. This, he said, gave us another avenue to explore.

I got a letter from Cam. He apologised for taking so long to get in touch, but was right behind me, and would gladly stand up in court for me. He said this could have happened to him because he had followed Surman-Wells and could have easily done something stupid like brick his window. He signed off, saying as soon as I got out we'd start planning our worldwide tour of festivals, starting with Fat Tuesday this September. Gregg sent word via Cam that he was rooting for me. I didn't expect a letter from him; it's not his style.

The trial date was set for 25th August – three months

away. As soon as I heard, I pictured the judge sentencing me to life and started to panic, and was put on suicide watch until I convinced them that all the blood was from the eczema on my arm.

Amber and I discussed the options put forward by Gallagher. I could go to trial, the outcome of which wasn't in doubt. I could change my plea and try and cop a deal for manslaughter, which would carry a five to eight-year sentence, provided the police went for it. Gallagher thought that they wouldn't, because they wanted the maximum sentence because of my criminal potential.

The final option was to try and prove I was unfit for trial. If I was found to be unfit for trial, I'd be treated in a secure hospital. The only problem with this, if we were successful, was that I wouldn't be serving any set sentence. Comparing my case to similar cases that had gone down this route, the time served averaged between three and five years. I would always be classed as a nut, maybe even an outpatient for life, but I had to seriously consider it because I was facing a life sentence.

Amber had broken down a few times as the net closed in on me. I had done myself, curling tight in a ball on the top bunk, silently crying for hours.

Gallagher had submitted three separate reports of my 'condition' from top psychologists and after nine months on remand, I was transferred to St Vincent's High Security Hospital for psychiatric assessment. It's the last thing the authorities wanted to sanction because they saw this as a clear-cut case and thought I was guilty of a whole lot more, so the reports had to be conclusive. We weren't claiming that I *didn't* kill him – only that I believed I didn't and was therefore mentally unstable at the time.

The psychologists we employed were of the opinion that I use avoidance suppression to blank out ordeals and replace them with self-protective thoughts. After comparing my version of a varying number of events with those of someone else's who was there (this was loosely confirmed from people working at Hargreaves Financial that knew me through my father, a child psychoanalyst who I saw when I was really young and one of my nannies), they found that my version was completely different. Large chunks of the event had been missed out and replaced with what I would have liked to have happened, or other memories dragged back in time to blank out the ordeal.

The child psychoanalyst also brought forward the strong possibility that I suffer panic and anxiety attacks, which turned out be an integral part of my case.

Amber told them how she had found me the night I bricked Surman-Wells' window. *He was distant and lost, sat clutching his arm, blood dripping onto the ground. He never spoke for ages. He was exhausted and frightened and in need of a cuddle.*

The psychologists at St Vincent's Hospital assessed me over a three-month period and concluded that I suffered from anxiety and panic attacks, had an obsessive personality and was very confrontational. They also said that in testing circumstances, it was likely I would become violent. All this based on the fact I was none too chuffed when they cancelled a visit from Amber at the last minute and wouldn't let me call her. They also agreed with the other psychologists, that I truly believed that I hadn't killed Surman-Wells.

I'd been in St Vincent's Hospital for three-and-half months when a small article about my case appeared in The Sydney Morning Herald and brought me to the attention of Karl Taylor. Karl Taylor was the kid that tried to rape Amber. I didn't deny fighting with him, only that he started it and I couldn't remember what actually happened in the fight, which is true. Ask anyone who's been in a proper tear up and they'll tell you the same: can't remember a thing. Karl Taylor had been in intensive care and his face was unrecognisable. Two of his mates were also hospitalised that night with facial injuries.

Anyway, that sealed my fate. They said I had an anti-social personality disorder. I looked it up in the dictionary. Individuals with anti-social personality disorder are aggressive and their behaviour is often irresponsible and unlawful, showing a disregard of social conventions.

If someone tried to rape your girlfriend before your very eyes, you would become very anti-social, too fucking right you would; you'd be straight into them with everything you had, wouldn't you? And most people would become paranoid and act out of character if they were being followed. All I'm saying is that given the right circumstances, we'd all have anti-social personality disorders.

They also said I had shown signs of psychopathy because I hadn't shown any remorse for my crimes or empathy for my victims. How can I show empathy for the fucker that tried to rape Amber? And how can I show remorse for Charles Surman-Wells when I hadn't even met him?

Anyway, we got the result and the judge sent me to St Vincent's Hospital, indefinitely.

23

I co-operated fully with the doctors and psychiatrists, but after a while the one-to-ones became less frequent and I spent more and more time in the dayroom with the nutters. I counted a straight eighteen days without any member of staff having direct contact with me – apart from one of the nurses, Ian, a young lad about twenty-six, who looked like the Milky Bar Kid. He chatted with me in the mornings when he unlocked my door and took me to the dayroom. He reckoned that even when it appeared nothing was happening, I was still being monitored and it was an important part of the recovery process.

The months dragged by and I became increasingly frustrated.

After one session with a psychiatrist I broke down crying, admitting for the millionth time that I had broken into 154 Palmer Street and confronted Surman-Wells and then attacked him. It was after this session, sitting back in my room, looking out over the gardens, that I realised I'd made the biggest mistake of my life. That I was in a situation I could never get out of. You see, the psychiatrists say they know when I'm lying.

They know when I'm telling them something I think they want to hear, and until I tell them from the heart what really happened, my recover cannot begin. If telling the truth is the only way I can make progress, then I can only tell them that I didn't do it. If I tell them that, the evidence says otherwise, and they don't believe me.

I went through this with Amber and the two of us cried all afternoon. I'm twenty-one-years-old and face spending the rest of my life in a nut-house.

Keith Gallagher had distanced himself from me, which left me only two options: escape and go on the run, or beg for help. I decided to beg for help. I told them the truth, that I didn't think I had done it and if I had, I wanted them to help me. Help me remember. Apparently, this is what they had been waiting for.

I was expecting electric shock treatment, something radical, but all they wanted to do was shut me off from the outside world for a month. No letters, phone calls, visits, nothing.

25

I couldn't settle and paced around a lot, checking out the windows to see if Amber was at the fence. I awoke at 12.15 every night and stared at the gates expecting to see Teatime's tail swishing around her shins.

Ian was the only member of staff that spoke to me. Halfway through the second week I couldn't even be bothered with him.

I sat at the window, counting the minutes down.

The four weeks passed.

Amber and I had arranged that I would ring her at nine sharp, she was taking the day off especially. Her mobile was out of service. I tried the flat number: no answer. I sloped off and joined the back of the queue.

I rang the flat on the hour all day.

I checked my post the next day, expecting a backlog of letters from her, like I had in my room, but there were none. After another frantic day on the phone, I realised what was happening. They, and Amber must be playing along, had cut her off 'for real' to see how I'd react.

A week past and Ian checked with the psychiatrists, and they said she was free to come and see me.

The phones were bothering me. They could stop my

mail and Amber visiting easy enough, but the phones? I rang Buckley, got through and asked him to check Amber's number. When I rang him back the fucker wouldn't take my call.

It took me a while and after switching and re-switching phone cards with other patients, I sussed out how they were doing it.

I was next in line.

The lad in front finished his call and walked away.

I waited.

Then, simultaneously, I grabbed the receiver, stuck it to my ear and looked over at Sarah in the tuck shop. I heard two loud clicks and Sarah lifted her eyebrows, like I'd caught her doing something. The fuckers were diverting my calls to Amber. I was probably ringing a number somewhere else in the building.

How long could they legally keep us apart?

I had this out with Ian the next day, and he said that my conspiracy theory made me sound like some of the more *permanent* patients. He suggested that maybe my girlfriend had had enough.

Four weeks passed and my daily routine never changed. Up, on the phone, sit down and write her a letter, rejoin the phone queue. Others in the day room had started calling me Buzby and shouting "it's for youhoooo" every time I came into the room. I didn't give a shit.

One afternoon, I was sat in the day room in my chair

next to the window. It had been raining all day. Half the window was steamed up. I watched the rain build up on the rubber seal, then spill over and run to the bottom. I was reminiscing about the robbery when I spotted someone at the gates.

I jumped up, pressing my face against the window. It was Amber in her blue hooded jacket, red on the sleeve, walking back and forth, Teatime sticking to her side. I ran round to the nurse on duty and demanded to be let out into the garden, that someone was here to see me. He wouldn't let me out so I grabbed his keys and tried to snap them off his waist, pulling him towards the door. I wrestled him to the floor and ripped his pants off at the ankles.

Before I could get the key in the lock, the other nurses arrived and sedated me.

In the dayroom I always sat next to the window with my back to everyone. It was the only way I'd know if Amber had been. It reminded me of being at home, looking out onto Mill Lane. A couple of times I got wound up thinking about Amber and had to be taken away to get my arm seen to. I explained about the eczema, but no one was really bothered. They just wanted me cleaned up and back in front of the window so I didn't cause any trouble.

A new starter, on his very first day, sat in my seat. I had a word and he moved away. The next day, I caught him staring at me in the dayroom. I heard he was carrying so I dropped a palette knife out of the window during art and picked it up later.

The following day, I waited in the dayroom for him. When it got to lunchtime, I went looking for him. I couldn't find him in any of the classes and his room was locked.

I found out later that he had been transferred.

I didn't know how long they intended to keep me like this or how long I could put up with it, but that morning they pushed me too far and I decided to revoke our agreement. I'd made up my mind. I wanted to go back to prison and stand trial for murder. At least that way I'd be serving a set sentence. The way things were, I couldn't see me ever getting out of there.

Today was their last throw of the dice to fuck me up and it didn't work.

I was in my room waiting for Ian, holding the letter I received that morning. The letter was from Amber.

Dear Spence,

I hope the treatment is going well. I've been doing a lot of thinking in the time we've been apart, and I think, maybe, oh, I don't know what I think. It's just that, after speaking with the doctors it might be best if we didn't see each other for a while. I mean, more than a while. For good. I'm so sorry, and I can hardly write these words but I think we will both be better off without each other, especially you. They say you need time alone, to, you know, find the problem, and start getting better and

I'm an outside influence and, well, you know it's for the best. I'm so sorry. I'm doing this for you.

I'll always love you, Spence.

Love A xx

I very nearly fell for it. Fuck me, I was so close to being taken in because it sounded just like her, the words used were the same as hers, but they made one glaring mistake – one only Amber and I could spot. We sign off every letter with three kisses. Always. That's how many times we kissed each other in quick succession that first night in the park. HER-ME-HER. KISS-KISS-KISS

Ian unlocked my door.

I was standing in the corner, letter behind my back.

He came in and picked up my flip chart. "So," he said, taking a pen from his top pocket. "What's on the agenda today?"

I stepped towards him and held up the letter. "First up. I want to know who –"

"Wrote this letter?" He sighed and sat down on the corner of my bed. He took his glasses off, pinched his nose and muttered, "Jesus, God."

"Then I want to –"

"Speak to my brief?"

"That's, eh, right."

Ian looked dejected that morning and I suggested that maybe he was doing too many hours.

"It's not that, Spence," he said, running his hands

through his hair and putting his glasses back on. "Do you know how hard this job is? When you came in here, you were no different to me. Now... now, you're..."

"I know what they're trying to do, Ian. That's why I want you to sort it so I can see Gallagher."

"Everyday see Gallagher and get sorted." Ian stood up. "What's it going to be, Spence? Hand the letter over to me and spend the day in the dayroom, or be sedated and left in here?"

"Eh? What you on about, sedated? Are you telling me," I stepped up to him and he backed away, "that you know nothing about this letter?"

"Spencer, you got to let it go."

"So you know nothing about this letter?"

Ian looked at me, then at the alarm button on the wall.

"Tell me you know this isn't from her."

"Look, Spencer, take it easy."

"Tell me you know this isn't from her."

He edged away.

"Tell me you know this isn't from her."

He hit the alarm and lunged for the door.

I kicked it shut and smashed my head into the glass.

"Tell me you know this isn't from her!"

With the footsteps and voices nearly upon me, I reached under my mattress for my blade.

PaperBooks

This book has been published by vibrant publishing company Paperbooks. If you enjoyed reading it then you can help make it a major hit. Just follow these three easy steps:

1. Recommend it

Pass it onto a friend to spread word-of-mouth or, if now you've got your hands on this copy you don't want to let it go, just tell your friend to buy their own or maybe get it for them as a gift. Copies are available with special deals and discounts from our own website and from all good bookshops and online outlets.

2. Review it

It's never been easier to write an online review of a book you love and can be done on Amazon, Waterstones.com, WHSmith.co.uk and many more. You could also talk about it or link to it on your own blog or social networking site.

3. Read another of our great titles

We've got a wide range of diverse modern fiction and it's all waiting to be read by fresh-thinking readers like you! Come to us direct at www.legendpress.co.uk to take advantage of our superb discounts. (Plus, if you email lucyboguslawski@legend-paperbooks.co.uk just after placing your order and quote 'WORD OF MOUTH', we will send another book with your order absolutely free!)

Thank you for being part of our word-of-mouth campaign.

www.paperbooks.co.uk